QUITE A YEAR FOR PLUMS

ALSO BY BAILEY WHITE

Mama Makes Up Her Mind
Sleeping at the Starlite Motel

Quite a Year
for Plums

A NOVEL

BAILEY WHITE

DOUBLEDAY DIRECT LARGE PRINT EDITION

ALFRED A. KNOPF NEW YORK 1998

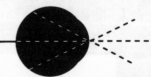

**This Large Print Book carries the
Seal of Approval of N.A.V.H.**

FOR ALBERT,
WITH MUCH GRATITUDE, ADMIRATION,
AND AFFECTION

CONTENTS

x Contents

CHARACTERS

Roger—a plant pathologist specializing in foliar diseases of peanut

Ethel—Roger's ex-wife, a schoolteacher

Louise—Ethel's mother

Eula—Louise's sister; Ethel's aunt

Tom—Eula's son, a forester. He is divorced from his wife Judy, who lives in California with their son Andy.

Andy—Tom's son. He spends summers in Georgia with his father and his grandmother Eula.

Hilma—a retired schoolteacher who taught with Ethel during her last ten years in the classroom

Meade—Hilma's best friend, also a retired schoolteacher

Gawain—an old forester

Lewis—an ornithologist studying the endangered red-cockaded woodpecker

Della—a wildlife artist visiting the area to study and paint local birds

Bruce—a vacationing typographer

Jim Wade—a collector of electric desk fans

Lucy—a nematologist

QUITE A YEAR FOR PLUMS

1. AGRISEARCH

The spring edition of *Agrisearch* came out with a picture on the front page of Roger standing in the middle of a field holding a peanut plant in each hand. In the distance you could see the irrigation rig behind him, and then the uneven line of trees at the back of the field. The caption said, "U. of Ga. plant pathologist Roger Meadows compares a peanut plant stunted and damaged by the tomato spotted wilt virus (left) with a healthy plant."

For some reason the picture had come out amazingly good in every respect. The frail, sickly plant on the left looked almost weightless, as if it were just hovering between life and death in Roger's tender grasp, while the robust plant on the right seemed aggressively healthy, its dark leaves outlined sharply against Roger's white shirt. The hand holding this plant was slightly lower, as if it were all a strong man could do to support the weight of such vigor.

Roger's friends were all so taken with the picture that they cut it out of their April *Agrisearch* and propped it up on windowsills or stuck it with magnets to the fronts of refrigerators.

At the Pastime Restaurant the waitresses taped the picture up on the wall beside the "In Case of Choking" poster. Betty, the cashier, wrote "This is Roger, in Albert Bateman's peanut field" on a takeout menu and taped it up under the picture.

Roger's old friend Meade made a mat for the picture out of faded red construction paper left over from her schoolteaching days. In her enthusiasm for accuracy and information, she penned in down at the bottom the date the photograph was taken; *Arachis hypo-*

gaea, the scientific name for peanut; and then 'Florunner,' the name of the cultivar.

Meade's friend and neighbor Hilma snipped Roger out of the peanut field with a pair of tiny scissors and transposed him onto two color photographs, so that he seemed to hover, artistically stark in *Agrisearch* black and white, between two lush springtimes—on the left, the bracken fern and longleaf pine woods on the hillside where his family house had once stood, and on the right, the 'Old Blush' in full bloom in his backyard rose garden.

Out in the country Roger's ex-wife's aunt Eula stuck the picture up on the refrigerator beside a crayon drawing of the *Titanic* her grandson had sent her from California. On the white of Roger's shirt Eula printed R-O-G-E-R in proud capital letters, with the final R dipping down out of consideration for the roots of the healthy peanut plant.

"As if anybody in this house doesn't know who that is," said her son Tom.

"Roger has such a kind face," said Hilma.

"And that well-bred nose," said Meade.

"Men's noses become so important when they lose their hair."

"They say you should always label your family pictures," Eula told Tom. "In a hundred years people will forget even Roger."

"Look a there, there's Roger on the icebox!" said Eula's sister Louise.

"Roger ain't family, Mama," said Tom. "Just because he picks the banjo with five fingers and married Ethel before he was old enough to know better, that don't make him family."

"R-O-G-E-R," said Louise. "They like a word like that, begins and ends with the same letter. But you got that last R so low, Eula, you got to be careful with your spacing, that can throw them off." For several years Louise had had the idea that spacemen were attracted to certain combinations of letters of the alphabet and certain arrangements of shapes and shiny objects, and this made her difficult to reason with at times.

"It's Roger, in *Agrisearch,* Louise, with his spotted wilt work," said Eula in a loud voice.

"Everywhere I go, there I am, me and those two peanut plants," said Roger.

"Fools' names and fools' faces." He and his nematologist friend Lucy were picking his first roses.

"It's just such a remarkable picture," said Lucy. "Everybody is struck by it. You look so deep, Roger. What in the world were you thinking about?"

"I was just feeling sorry for the photographer is all," said Roger. "He had driven all the way down here from Athens to take a picture of red wattle hogs in Sam Martin's new automatic feeder pens, but they couldn't get the doors to open, so the photographer said, 'Stand out in that field and hold up two peanut plants.' He had to come back the next week for the hogpens."

But even knowing that, people still prized their *Agrisearch* pictures of Roger in the peanut field.

"Just like Roger to be concerned about the photographer having that long drive for nothing," said Hilma.

"It is a remarkable likeness," said Meade. "It's his mother's nose."

"It was supposed to be two hogs, but they took a picture of Roger instead," Eula told Ethel on Saturday afternoon. But Ethel was looking at the foliage on the roses Roger had brought that morning.

"Roger knows how much I like the pink ones," said Eula, "so he always brings me 'Queen Elizabeth.'"

Ethel turned over a leaf and examined the back of it, but there were no spots on the leaves. "Nobody can grow roses like a plant pathologist," was all she said.

"He planted that rose garden just for her," said Meade, "because she loved them so, and before the 'Dr. W. Van Fleet' got to the top of the trellis she was gone." It was a perpetual conversation, why Ethel left Roger. Lucy and Meade were sitting on stools in Hilma's tiny kitchen watching her poke the stems of 'Madame Isaac Pereire' roses into a vase. The heads were floppy, which made them difficult to arrange, but Hilma loved the fragrance, so Roger saved 'Madame Isaac' for her.

"And for what?" Meade went on. "That little guitar-strumming nincompoop from Nashville with the wispy goatee, when Roger plays the banjo so beautifully. I will never understand Ethel."

"I don't think it had anything to do with

banjos or roses," said Lucy. "Ethel is just not domesticated, that's all."

"I saw it with my own eyes," said Meade. "She seduced him right off that stage."

"But we have all reaped the benefits of the rose garden Roger planted for Ethel," said Hilma, in an effort to stem the tide. "So we should not complain."

"Because she liked the way he tapped his feet," said Meade. "And poor Roger, left with nothing to comfort him but the Irish Potato Famine." For two years after Ethel had left him for the Nashville guitarist, Roger had immersed himself in a study of late blight of potato, and that look of resignation, wisdom, and patience had come into his face that was brought out so well in the *Agrisearch* photograph.

" 'I shall send upon you the evil arrows of famine,' " Meade quoted grimly, " 'and I will break your staff of bread.' "

"*Phytophthora infestens,* the Great Plant Destroyer," said Lucy. "The science of plant pathology had its beginnings in the Irish Potato Famine. It's very humbling to study a disease like that."

But all this seemed far too gloomy on

such a bright spring day, thought Hilma, with 'Madame Isaac' filling the room with its fragrance. It was not fair to blame Ethel for the Irish Potato Famine just because she had such a lively interest in a variety of men. "Ethel is a gifted teacher," she said. "That is an important thing to remember."

"I will never understand Ethel," said Meade. They sat for a minute, admiring that complex picture of Roger, looking so serious and thoughtful on Hilma's cupboard door. For all his *Agrisearch* wisdom and patience and resignation, still, at the corners of his mouth and in his eyes, squinting slightly in the sun, you could see just the beginning of a little smile, as if he had sense enough to realize that he did look slightly ridiculous, standing there to have his picture taken in the middle of a peanut field.

2. TOTAL CARE

"Let me call you back, Louise," Eula shouted into the telephone. "I've got a house full of men here, all wanting to be fed."

The men waiting to be fed were Eula's son Tom, a forester, and a southern pine beetle expert from North Carolina. Eula's niece Ethel was there too. She often came out to spend Saturday or Sunday afternoon with her aunt Eula in the country.

"You make them sound like baby birds, Aunt Eula," said Ethel.

"We should be cooking for you, Mrs. Matthews," said the ridiculously polite beetle expert.

"Oh, just sit down and eat," said Eula. And there was something about the way she paused for a moment at her place, gripping the back of her chair with both hands and glaring critically down at the laden table, that made it seem as if no one in the world had any business cooking food but Eula Matthews.

There was a dish of fried eggplant, a chipped enamel bowl of sliced tomatoes and Vidalia onions, a squash casserole, pole beans, corn bread, biscuits, and a jar of pickled okra.

"It's too hot to eat meat," said Eula. "You boys out in those sweltering woods all day, listening to grubs gnawing in those big trees. Ethel, get yourself some eggplant and pass it down to Tom."

After lunch the men wandered back out, talking about board feet, and Ethel said, "You're supposed to call Mama."

"I know what your mama wants to talk about, more of those little spacemen coming in the house," said Eula. She wrung out the dishrag and hung it over the edge of the sink, tugging the corners square. Then she leaned with her arms on the counter and looked out across Louise's neglected garden into the pasture.

"Just look at that Bahia grass going to seed," she said. Ethel didn't say anything, because when Eula started talking about grass it meant she was thinking about her husband Melvin, who had been horribly killed twenty years ago when his beloved old Allis-Chalmers tractor turned over on him when he was mowing a steep grassy slope. Finally she blew her nose on a paper towel and dialed the telephone.

"Last time they came in, Louise told me they painted the edges of her jalousie windows pale green," she said to Ethel. " 'Louise,' I said, 'those little men didn't paint those windows! That glass just is green on the edges.' But Louise thinks too much, that's what's wrong." Eula waited while the telephone rang on the other end. "I almost hate to hear this," she whispered to Ethel.

"Hey, Louise," she shouted. "I'm calling you back. Yeah, come on over, Ethel's here. Yeah, they're gone back in the woods, come on over. Yeah, bye.

"Unh unh," said Eula. "I worry about your mama, Ethel, the way she lets her mind get away from her. I put my address on her walking stick just in case she wanders too far, gets lost. She's going to wind up in town under Total Care at Shady Rest, my own baby sister, I can see it coming, Ethel."

Louise sat up earnestly on the edge of the sofa with her elbows on her knees. "It come in just as smooth," she said. "The ship was called the *Uncovered Eroticum*. It was one of those convertible-type spaceships, and, honey, let me tell you, the top was down." She pulled a crumpled foil chewing-gum wrapper out of her pocket and pressed it smooth. Then she laid a black plastic capital J on the coffee table so that the strip of foil stretched out from the top of the J like a flag.

"And then a swarm of little men got out, each one of them smaller than the one before. Eula, you will never believe what those men proceeded to do in my house."

Eula shouted, "Don't tell me, Louise, I don't want to know that!"

"You should have told them to come over here, Mama," said Ethel. "Aunt Eula would have fed them up and sent them out in the woods to measure timber."

"Child," said Louise, "those little men didn't want to be fed. Food is not what they were after."

"Don't talk about it, Louise!" Eula shouted. "Have a biscuit!"

"I've got a biscuit right here in my hand, Eula," said Louise. "If I was hungry I'd eat it."

"Louise," said Eula, "you keep letting your mind go off with you like that, one day it's not going to bring you back. You're going to wind up out there at Shady Rest with those quivering idiots."

A week later the beetle man from North Carolina found Louise wandering around in the woods, all scratched up and hungry, with two days' worth of redbug bites on her. The beetle man read the address on her walking stick and took her to Eula. Eula ran her a bath, gave her a bottle of Chiggerid, fed her a hot meal, and put her to bed. Ethel came out after school, and Eula's son Tom came in early from the woods, covered with seed ticks.

"She needs taking care of," said Tom to Ethel in a fierce voice. "She could have been snake bit." But Tom was standing in the middle of the living room floor in his underwear, glistening with the pine oil he had smeared on himself to kill the ticks, and it was hard to take him seriously.

"This ain't funny, Ethel!" said Tom. "This is your own mama's safety we're talking about!"

"I'm not laughing at Mama, Tom," said Ethel. "I'm laughing at you."

"I know what's going to happen, I can see it in my mind's eye right now," said Tom, and he marched around the living room rug in little circles on his greasy, high-arched feet. "You just watch: Louise is going to move in here with us, and Mama's going to be stuck with her, listening to all that crazy talk, looking after her like she was a little child, keeping her from wandering off. She's your mama, Ethel, you ought to be taking care of her!" He stopped and stood still in the middle of the rug and stared into space with his eyes wide open. "Yep, I can see it right now in my mind's eye, me and Mama and Louise crammed in here together, and Ethel all alone up there in that nice house on Dawson Street, teaching school."

"Tom, you don't need an eye in your mind to see that. We can all see that," said Eula. "Of course she's going to move in here with us. Louise can't live up there with Ethel. A crazy person can't live in town, she'd get out on the street when

Ethel's off at school, get run over, kid-napped, I don't know what all, they'd take her up to Milledgeville if they saw her in town, the way she is. Don't you worry about your mama, Ethel, and, Tom, go wash off, you're going to blister yourself with that pine oil."

"It almost made me cry, Roger," said Eula. It was the next Saturday. Ethel didn't have a truck, and Tom was at the longleaf pine conference at Wakulla Springs, so Ethel's ex-husband Roger was helping Eula move Louise's stuff. They were on their third load—dump, Goodwill, and now a load Louise said she had to keep. Eula had cleared out the back hall for it.

"My own baby sister, and she can't take care of herself. I felt tears in my eyes, Roger. Of course it could have been that pine oil on Tom, that'll make your eyes water when you're shut up with it."

"It probably wasn't just the pine oil," said Roger. "This is something worth cry-ing about. It's going to be hard on you, Eula."

"Oh, I'll be all right," said Eula. "I'm just worried about some things. Andy coming from California for the summer and all that spaceman talk, you know how Louise can get raw with it sometimes, a young boy hearing that, I don't know. And then the house—a house begins to go down when nobody's living in it. A house needs people walking around in it, talking, sleeping, putting off heat. And Tom, you know how he can be, and then there's . . ." But Roger knew she wasn't going to say anything to him about Ethel.

"I just wish it hadn't happened right in the middle of Mayhaw season," said Eula. "I've got three gallons of berries on the back porch right now."

Roger stopped in front of Louise's house and they sat for a minute. "One more load," he said.

"Looks like that porch is already beginning to sag, don't it, Roger?" said Eula.

"This is your home now, Louise," said Eula. "You've got to get used to it." But Louise was busy playing with jar lids and jar rings on the kitchen table, laying them out in patterns, ring lid lid, ring lid lid.

"Put a couple of 9's in there," she said, "and a u-p-s. Where are my big numbers, Eula?"

"And you've got to quit wandering off, Louise," said Eula. "The UPS man was nice to bring you back today; next time you might not be so lucky. I notice you're still scratching those redbug bites."

Eula was standing by the stove with a long wooden spoon waiting for the Mayhaw juice to come to a full rolling boil. "Louise, quit rubbing your fingers on the insides of those lids, they've been sterilized. Go get your big numbers, they're on the bottom shelf in the back hall, a couple of 6's, I saw a 9, letters too, capital and small. Roger put them on that low shelf so you can get to them."

It was after midnight before Eula got the jelly pot washed and the jelly bag rinsed and hung up to dry and the last twenty-four jars set upside down on a white cloth on the kitchen table. But still, she sat up for a few minutes to read her cowboy book and listen for the pleasing little popping sounds from the kitchen that meant the jar lids were making a perfect seal.

It might not be so bad, she thought. Roger said there were people from up north who would pay good money to rent Louise's house during the winter and spring. They would just have to cut a stack of firewood, is all. And Tom had settled down after Eula had a little talk with him. "It's hard to see your own mama go crazy," she had told him, and since then he hadn't said any more mean things about Ethel. Louise had stayed busy with her letters and numbers, and she hadn't mentioned the *Uncovered Eroticum* since she had moved in.

Eula lay in the bed and listened to the rustles and thumps in the back hall, and thought about the woman in the book she was reading, and how she would write poems on strips of paper and tie them onto tumbleweeds and let them blow away. Eula had never seen a tumbleweed, but she could just imagine how it would look tossing across that bare, dry land with the little strip of poem trailing off it like one of Louise's silver foil banners flying off the top of a capital J. In the end, that nice cowboy man Conn Conagher would marry the woman with the tumbleweeds, Eula knew that. She only liked books that had happy endings, so she always peeked, just to be sure.

3. UNMARRIED WOMEN

"Trollope," said Meade. "That dreary march through chapter after chapter, waiting for Plantagenet to be named Chancellor of the Exchequer."

It was late April, and Meade and Hilma were arguing about what book to read aloud on their Thursday Evenings in May. It was a ritual they had cheerfully observed since the early days of their friendship fifty years ago, when they had both been new teachers at the old Midway School. But this year they were wrangling.

"You only want to read the Palliser novels because you have an adolescent crush on Phineas Finn," Meade said.

Hilma sighed. Meade wanted to read *Emma,* although they had already read *Emma* in May of '79 and again in May of '85. It was true that Hilma had a soft spot in her heart for Phineas Finn, but it didn't seem fair that Meade's love for Mr. Knightley counted as a loftier emotion than hers for Phineas, more literary in tone.

"You know, of course," said Meade, "that the character of Mr. Knightley is one of the most finely drawn in literature."

And suddenly Hilma felt sick to death of Mr. Knightley and Emma and Meade and all of the Thursday Evenings in May. "Why do we shut ourselves up in this little room anyway, and read aloud in the month of May, when the ferns in the woods are unfurling, and the lightning bugs are coming out in swarms? We should be doing something daring, with action and adventure," she blurted out desperately.

" 'And why do we read anyway, when the lightning bugs are swarming?' I said to Meade, and then she said in that challenging way, 'Exactly what did you have in mind?' But of course, Ethel, I didn't have anything specific in mind, just not *Emma* for the third time," Hilma said to Ethel the next day. They had taught first grade to-gether too, for Ethel's first and Hilma's last ten years. It had been nothing for the two of them to figure out how to make the inside of a shoe box look exactly like the Okefenokee Swamp in a few moments of whispered consultation in a darkened classroom at rest time, so it was natural for Hilma to come to Ethel with the dilemma of the Thursday Evenings in May. "Meade is my oldest and dearest friend, Ethel, but she can be so difficult at times."

"The sap is rising," said Ethel. "You are feeling restless, that's all. It's spring. You need a change." And she handed Hilma a book off her shelf: Bartram's *Travels.*

"Come with me on Saturday to the Fountain of Youth," she said.

"Fountain of Youth," said Meade to Roger. "Action and adventure. Ethel has taken her off to central Florida, where they are to bathe in one of the springs near the spot where William Bartram ate tripe soup with the Seminole chief Cowkeeper in May of 1774. My oldest and dearest friend will probably be swallowed up by one of those giant central Florida alligators, and all because I didn't want to spend my Thursday Evenings in May reading about the Duke of Omnium's great campaign for the five-farthinged penny."

"The dangers of central Florida have changed since 1774," said Roger. "I don't think the alligators will bother them."

"Still," said Meade, " I do hope Ethel will look after her. Hilma is not as strong as she pretends to be."

" 'Two very large ones attacked me closely' "—Ethel was driving nearly 80 miles per hour down I-75 and reciting her favorite passages from Bartram's *Travels* by heart—" 'roaring terribly and belching floods of water over me. They struck their jaws together so close to my ears as to almost stun me, and I expected at every moment to be dragged out of the boat and instantly devoured.' "

But Hilma couldn't keep her mind on alligators. She kept noticing the billboards rearing up out of the cow pastures along the side of the road—a skimpily dressed, dyspeptic-looking young woman nine feet high, and the great words towering against the blue sky: WE BARE ALL. Hilma thought wistfully of the familiar comforts of the Thursday Evenings in May, Mr. Woodhouse with his basin of thin gruel and his frettings about the damp and the dirt and the dangers of sea air. It's spring, and the sap is rising, Ethel had said, but when they finally pulled into the sandy parking lot and heard through the woods the splashes and screams of the spring bathers, Hilma just sat in the car, feeling vulnerable and frail. Now when she thought of sap she remembered the morning sun shining through the chunk of amber she kept on a windowsill at home, and the little million-year-old fly frozen inside, with its bent and folded wings and its crumpled little legs.

" 'The waters appear of a lucid sea green color,' " Ethel recited, gathering up towels and canvas bags of swimming gear. She stood patiently, holding the car door open for Hilma. " 'The ebullition is perpendicular upwards from a vast ragged orifice through a bed of rocks.' " And sure enough, around a shady bend in the sandy trail and through the woods, there it was—the Fountain of Youth.

It was dazzling—the brightness of the

clear water, the deep new green of the surrounding vegetation, and the turquoise blue of the little spring and its river. The white sand glittered.

" 'It is amazing and almost incredible, what troops and bands of fish and other water inhabitants are now in sight,' " quoted Ethel.

But there were no fish in sight. The only water inhabitants were people, splashing and shrieking in the shallows or floating down the crystal stream belly-down in inner tubes, their bare feet poking stiffly toward the sky like ghastly plants struggling for sunlight. Something about the sun and the bright clear water and the luxuriant vegetation made the people look vivid and surreal, the white people whiter, the hairy people hairier, the stringy people stringier.

"My goodness," said Hilma, but Ethel had left the canvas bags in a heap on the shore and was gone. Hilma could see her little head bobbing in the water where she floated, twirling slowly around and around over the boil. Every now and then a little burst of spray would shoot up from her snorkel.

Hilma took her shoes off and waded in

gingerly up to her knees, poking at the sandy bottom with the tip of her walking stick. But little sharp rocks gouged her feet and the water was so cold it burned, and after just a minute she crept out. She wrung out her dress tail and carefully spread a towel on the grass in a little glade and sat, hugging her knees. She could feel a sweet aching in her legs and feet from the cold, and the bright glare, the distant shouts of the bathers, and the greenness made her feel dizzy or sleepy, and after a minute she closed her eyes and let her mind wander. For a while she thought about the sleazy motel near exit 73 where she and Ethel were to spend the night. Would there be a hair of the previous guest in the yellowed fiberglass bathtub? Would there be a dark and mysterious stain on the orange shag carpet? Would she and Ethel be able to sleep with the bright lights blinking WE BARE ALL through the thin curtains, or, worse, would they both be raped and strangled in their lumpy beds by lusty revelers from the Café Risqué across the road? Then she thought about Phineas Finn. It was in just such a place of great natural beauty as this, at the top of the falls of the Linter, that he had proposed to Lady Laura Standish in that touching way of his, looking as handsome as a god in his velvet shooting jacket, and kissed her.

When Hilma opened her eyes she saw an old man standing beside her, eating a thin sandwich on white bread. His skin was so pale it looked almost translucent, and his feet were so stringy and knobby that they looked more like mechanical models of feet than real flesh and blood. He stood, chewing his sandwich and looking down into the water for a long time. Then he said, "This your first time to the spring?"

"Yes," said Hilma in her best schoolteacher voice, "although I have read about this spring. The great naturalist and explorer William Bartram visited here in 1774."

"Lot of folks come with their families—husbands, wives, the kids," the old man said, "to ride the tubes." He took a step closer, and Hilma watched the strings in the tops of his feet tighten and loosen.

"Myself," he said, "I'm not a married man." He took a bite of his sandwich and chewed thoughtfully. Then he asked, "Are you a married woman?"

Hilma sprang up, snatched her towel off the ground, and flapped it viciously between them. "Sir!" she said. "That is not a civilized question!"

"I was just thinking," he said. "They say this spring has powers. And you being here all by yourself and me being an unmarried man, well, I was just thinking, why—"

This time the water didn't feel as cold, and she floundered in deeper and deeper, clutching her skirt with both hands, until she stepped off a little rocky ledge and plunged in over her head. There was the first gasp when she thought she had died, and then, as she began to swim, the gulps for air became more moderate, and she could feel the coldness gradually seeping into her, until the only warmth she had left came from deep inside, and she imagined that she could make out the shapes of her internal organs by their heat: her foamy lungs and her flaccid liver with the little green gallbladder, hot and dense, nestling beneath it. Underwater there was no sound, just color and light. Even the wild dance of the eelgrass in the turbulent surge seemed peaceful in all that silence, and every time she lifted her head to take a breath it was startling to hear a second's burst of sound, like a yelp or a bleat. Hilma floated and gasped and floated and gasped, with her eyes open wide, until Ethel paddled up beside her, and together they climbed out and sat on the bank with their teeth chattering. Hilma wanted to tell Ethel about the flight from the unmarried man, the icy plunge, and how in that silent green and silver world she had felt the last of her anger at Meade and Mr. Knightley seep away along with her body heat until all she could feel was one tiny spot of warmth somewhere near her spleen. But they were both too cold to speak and they just sat on the sand, shivering and grinning.

"They are spending the night in Micanopy, near the site where Bartram frolicked with Indian maidens," said Meade, heaping mashed potatoes on Roger's plate, "across the road from the Café Risqué, where, I understand, women prance around on the countertops stark naked while men eat sloppy joes and poke dollar bills at them through a chain-link fence."

"I didn't know the part about the chain-link fence," said Roger.

They sat for a while, eating their civilized meal with a dinner fork and a salad fork, and listened to coffee percolating in the kitchen.

"I do hope Hilma is getting enough to eat," said Meade. "Ethel is not apt to remember simple things like food."

The Café Risqué, painted glossy purple and white, sat in the very center of its shimmering asphalt parking lot surrounded by bright spotlights on tall poles. Fake turquoise shutters framed blank spaces on the walls, and signs had been painted where there might have been windows:

NUDE DANCING
"ADULT TOY" GIFT SHOP
GREAT FOOD!
24-HOUR CAMERA
SURVEILLANCE

"I can tell by your sunburn you been in the spring," the woman in the motel office said. "You had a nice day for it. Yep, that's mostly who we get in here, tubers." She wagged her head toward the Café Risqué and raised her eyebrows at Hilma. "And them. The tubers, at least they're clean, been in that icy water all day, and quiet, wore out from all that paddling. Them, they're mostly truckers."

The room was shabby but clean. There was no stained carpet and no stray hair in the bathroom, just worn-out linoleum and a row of cigarette burns on the edge of the tub.

Ethel was hungry, and as soon as they had gotten settled in, she went off toward Micanopy to try to find something to eat, but Hilma just wanted to sit still and savor the salubrious effects of an afternoon spent in the Fountain of Youth. She lay on the threadbare sheet on the bed beside the window and watched the Café Risqué grow brighter and brighter as the night came on until it almost seemed to blaze with light. Just like the orchids you see on educational television, she thought, luring species-specific pollinators with elaborate tricks of mimicry. And right before she fell asleep she remembered with pleasure the name the Indians had given William Bartram: Puk Puggy—the Flower Hunter.

4. A NICE DAY

It was late May, housecleaning season, when Roger fell in love with a woman at the dump. He never saw her. He just liked the way she threw things away. Sometimes she left clothes draped gracefully across a corner of the Dumpster—a nicely laundered shirt, its long sleeves tucked up away from a rusty patch, or a pair of blue jeans folded across slightly worn knees. Sometimes she put things off to the side, arranged in orderly rows in the grassy ditch at the edge of the woods—a white plastic fan, a ceramic container of wooden spoons, a clip-on bedside light, and a whole hummingbird cake wrapped in several layers of plastic wrap and aluminum foil, set up on a stump. She left notes on some items.

"This fan works, but it makes a clicking sound and will not oscillate."

"I can't eat this whole hummingbird cake."

And Roger's favorite, taped to a Hamilton Beach fourteen-speed blender: "Works good."

He admired the style of the notes, the generous margins, the almost childish legibility, the careful use of punctuation, and the casual and almost intimate "good" instead of the grammatical but pretentious "well." He was intrigued by the skewed logic in some of the notes, where her mind seemed to go skittering away from reason and fact, in a direction he could almost follow, but not quite:

"If you are tall, maybe this light won't shine in your eyes."

"I'm intrigued," he said to Hilma and Meade, who both seemed horrified. "How many people do you know who can spell 'oscillate'?" he asked. "I admire good spellers."

"O-s-c-i-double l-a-t-e," snapped Meade.

"But, Roger," said Hilma sensibly, "she could be a racist or a thief. She could be cruel to animals. You can't draw conclusions about a person based on nothing more than a fourteen-speed blender and a white plastic fan."

"No," said Roger, "of course not." But still he made a point of stopping by the Dumpster every time he went to Attapulgus to do his thrips counts, just checking. She threw away a radio/tape player: "Squawking in left speaker will stop if you tap the volume knob." She threw away two plastic chairs.

The absence of things can give a kind of shape to a space, and using his collection of negatives, Roger imagined the inside of her house, silent, light, and spare, without a cheap white fan clicking but not oscillating, without the high scream of an electric blender on Whip, without the ridiculous excess of a hummingbird cake. He imagined her in the house, padding silently from room to room on big bare feet, looking for things to throw away.

* * *

Della had come to south Georgia to make a yearlong study of her special birds—coots, gallinules, and rails—in the spring-fed rivers and swamps and the salt marshes at the coast. But instead of beginning that serious work, she had found herself falling under the spell of a small flock of chickens at a nearby hatchery.

"America's oldest breed of chickens, ma'am, now endangered," the poultryman had told her, looking sorrowfully at the big black and white birds scratching in the dust. "A hundred years ago every family had three or four Dominickers in the backyard, and now you can count the registered flocks on one hand." Before she had even settled into her small apartment, Della had begun a large watercolor painting of a brace of Dominiques and thrown away most of her household goods.

In the early sketching phase she threw out the fan because the clicking disrupted her concentration. But there was something so satisfying about setting that cheap white fan down in the grass by the Dumpster and driving away from it that a few days later, when the work became more difficult, she threw out several electrical appliances. And when she began the feathers, a week of dizzying black and white, requiring such a light touch, delicate but not tentative, she threw out all of her kitchen utensils and most of her furniture. She ate cold food from the grocery store out of its plastic wrap, standing over the kitchen sink, and in the evenings, with her head aching slightly from eyestrain, she walked downtown to the Pastime Restaurant and ordered a vegetable plate.

If the work had gone well that day, she would linger over her greasy beans and new potatoes and then sit peacefully for a while, smiling to herself and enjoying the dense white of the old china plates at the Pastime, the shallow dishes of pickles on each table, and the waitresses, who seemed so different from her, big and loud and friendly.

On other days, she would grip her knife and fork in her fists and stab her food around, and then she would shove the whole thing away and make little sketches of difficult bits of the painting on the back of the place mat. When she got home she would pace around and around her apartment ferociously, and pile up stuff by the door to throw away.

It was on one of these bad nights that she first noticed the picture of Roger and the two peanut plants. She was looking at it when Betty handed her her change and said, "You have a nice day now." But it was nine o'clock at night, she was stuck on the scaly yellow legs of the Dominique rooster, and when she got home she threw away a telephone and a small space heater. It was not a nice day.

"She's strange," said Betty. "She's got a gone look in her eyes."

Then Fern, who was clearing off tables, called out, "Look at this! Chicken feet!" Some were flat on the ground, toeing inward slightly; some were taking a step, walking or running; some were flung up, toes outspread, with threatening spurs. Fern and Betty sat down at the booth surrounded by dirty dishes and examined the place mat, turning it around and around to see the chicken feet.

"Now if she can draw that good, why in the world does she want to draw chicken feet?" said Fern. "Seems like she'd want to be drawing a vase of flowers or a man on a horse."

"She's strange, I told you," said Betty.

"You have a nice day now," Della whispered the next morning as she sat on her little stool at the hatchery, watching the four Dominiques scratch and peck and strut and wallow in the dust.

"You have a nice day now," she whispered to herself all afternoon as she sat at her drawing table, staring at her brushes with her hands in her lap.

"You're the one drew them good chicken feet last night," said Fern, shoving the salt and pepper and sugar jar to one side and wiping down the table with a rag. "I don't know what else you can draw, but you can sure draw some chicken feet, honey. Me and Betty both said that, we said, 'She might be a little strange, but she knows she can draw chicken feet.' Now what you want to eat tonight?" And she bunched the rag up in a discreet little wad on the corner of the table and stood there, clutching her pad against her bosom and making little scribbling movements above it with the nub of a pencil. But Della just sat, seeing her troubled, secret life with the chickens laid open in the bright light of the Pastime Restaurant by this boisterous, big-faced woman smelling slightly of Clorox.

"Now what you want to eat tonight, honey, your regular?" asked Fern in a louder voice, and she snatched up the rag and went away, leaving Della staring at the red glowing letters spelling e-m-i-t-s-a-P against the black window.

"You some kind of a chicken artist?" asked Betty at the cash register, but it alarmed Della to be called any kind of artist at all with the painting going so badly, and fumbling in her pocketbook for the correct change, she said, "Well, no, not now, I guess, although—really, no." When she looked up with her two pennies and a quarter, there it was, that nice day with the magnificent white clouds and the line of trees at the back of the field and the bald-headed man with the kind face holding those plants so carefully.

"You have a nice day, honey," said Betty.

For the rest of the week everything she tried to paint came out dense and muddy. It was ridiculous to think that she could make out of black paint, water, and white paper those shimmering barred feathers, where the black and the white seemed to switch places with every blink of the eye, and one night at the cash register when Betty asked, "So how are my chickens coming?" Della took a deep breath and held it, and then covered her face with both hands. Fern put down her stack of dishes and thumped her on the back hard, several times.

"Why, I know chickens ain't easy, honey, they ain't got no shape to them." She peeled several napkins off the to-go stack and poked them in between Della's clenched fingers. "I know what," she said, and she closed her eyes and sucked on her lip thoughtfully. "You go home and sit down and paint you a little house. Put a flower garden out front, paint you a little man out there in it with a hoe. If you want to put a bird in it, put a bird in it," and she clapped Della on the back to comfort her. "Just don't paint no chickens in there."

Then Betty came bustling out of the back with a big white frozen lump wrapped up in plastic. "Here," she said, "you take this home, it's a hummingbird cake."

They were such kind gifts, the little man with the hoe and the frozen cake, and Della wanted to smile and say something grateful, but the black and white that kept flashing in her head made her woozy and she didn't trust herself to speak. She stood there at the cash register, staring at the picture of the peanut field, her eyes aching from the black and white and her arms aching from the frozen cake, while Betty and Fern glanced back and forth furtively.

"Honey," Betty said at last, "that's nothing but Roger in the spring *Agrisearch* with his spotted wilt work."

"Thank you so much," said Della, "for everything. It's so kind of you, I shouldn't really, I can't . . ." And before Betty could say "Have a nice day," she had left her $4.95 on the counter and was gone. The cake must have weighed ten pounds.

"Little studies," she called them. A stick and a leaf, a single pinecone, a striped gourd, an acorn beside its cap, nothing bigger than five by seven. "They'll do me good," she told herself with forced cheerfulness, and she slid the unfinished chicken painting into the middle of a stack of new paper and taped it up. Every morning she sat at her table under the light, painting tiny single things on cheap paper, and every afternoon she gathered them up, looked them over, and threw them away.

Sometimes people are uneasy when they meet strangers at Dumpsters beside country roads, miles from a town— the dark woods in the background, the sinister-looking shiny black bags, frightening glittery things in the sand, the closest building a deserted church on a hill around the bend—so Roger stood back to give her a comfortable distance and waited while she squatted in the mud, lining her little paintings up against the flange at the base of the Dumpster.

When she finally stood up and turned around, she looked so sad and troubled that Roger had to stop himself from stepping forward to comfort her. She just stood there for a long time, staring at him, and then all of a sudden she smiled and laughed out loud and said, "Have a nice day!"

5. TOSSING FLOWERS INTO THE SWAMP

"I certainly hope there are not ticks," said Hilma, trying to keep her feet on the rungs of her chair. Her suggestion for the new adventurous Thursdays in May Evenings had been to eat chilled food in her backyard, where her night-blooming garden was just coming into flower— Datura, four-o'clocks, Nicotiana, and moonvine in a round bed. But Meade had taken Ethel's suggestion about the rising sap literally. "The smell of pine sap will open your mind," she had said.

And so there they were on a cool late May evening, two old women sitting in chairs in the middle of a thousand acres of longleaf pine woods. Meade had not wanted to bring anything but the chairs—"The idea is to be unencumbered"—but Hilma had brought dishes of custard in a canvas bag. "You can't enjoy being unencumbered if you are hungry," she said. They would stay until dark, breathing the piney air and watching the lightning bugs come out.

He stood on a little rill and looked across at them through his binoculars. It seemed odd, two women sitting in the middle of the woods in rocking chairs. But then, he spent so much time in the woods himself, studying the intricate and complex behavior of one rare and elusive little bird, that almost everything about people seemed odd to him, the things they said and did, the clothes they wore, the shoes they put on their feet.

Two rocking chairs, not matched. One had a cushion, one had a straight ladder back. They were eating something white with spoons. Two old women in the middle of the woods in rocking chairs. He would have to ask Gawain about it.

* * *

"Must be Meade and Hilma," said Gawain. He and the ornithologist were looking at a map of a large tract of woods, Gawain's 600 acres of mixed loblolly, longleaf, and slash pine, and Roger's neighboring 350 acres of almost pure longleaf. Tiny circles indicated the biggest redheart trees, irregular loops enclosed areas of extensive longleaf reseeding, and dots marked the location of woodpecker activity—blue for an inactive roost cavity, red for a roost in use this season. Gawain was an expert on controlled burning, and these endangered woodpeckers were a fire-dependent species.

"They go and sit in the woods every Thursday afternoon?" the ornithologist asked.

But it was hard to get any conversation with Gawain off the subject of fire in the woods. "Take this area of young longleaf, February of the year 1978, those seedlings hadn't been sprouted four months, Roger put a cool fire through there, now that's the finest stand of young longleaf in the county. We just have one word for it, 'fire,' but fire is a billion things, Lewis, and in the hands of a knowledgeable forester, it can be a delicate and precise tool."

"These old ladies, they—"

"Two old-lady retired schoolteachers," said Gawain, "but they understand the uses of fire, both of them."

"Here comes a man through the woods," said Meade, "with a pair of spyglasses around his neck." It was the last Thursday in May; the bracken fern was almost four feet high, and sitting in their rocking chairs, Hilma and Meade were almost concealed by greenery.

"Maybe we should call out," said Hilma, "so he won't come upon us unexpectedly and be startled."

Meade raised a hand above the ferns. "Hello! Hello!" she called out. But the man was not surprised. He walked right up to them and stood there for a minute, clutching his binoculars with both hands, his head thrust slightly forward.

"We can't offer you a seat," said Meade. "We didn't expect you, and we only have these two chairs."

But even in the middle of a thousand acres of open woodland Hilma felt the responsibilities of a hostess, as if this strange young man in his worn canvas boots were an uncomfortable guest needing to be put at ease. "My name is Hilma and this is my friend Meade," she said. There was a pause. "What is your name?" Hilma prompted.

"Oh," he said, adjusting the focus on his binoculars with convulsive little thrusts of both thumbs. "Lewis."

"And," Hilma went on, "with those field glasses you must be making a close observation of something. I would be interested to know what that might be."

"Oh," said the young man, and as if he had just been given life, he began to move and speak. He squatted down at their feet and then stood back up and looked up into the trees and pointed in the distance to things they could not see, talking all the while about red-cockaded woodpeckers: their nesting habits, their complicated social structure, their need for open longleaf woods, and his own cooperative-behavior study showing the role of helper males from previous generations in raising each year's new fledglings. ". . . the healthiest RCW population outside of the Apalachicola Forest," he concluded.

Meade and Hilma listened intently,

leaning forward in their chairs. "Why," said Hilma, "I never! I have only seen a red-cockaded woodpecker once in my life when Roger pointed, and you have learned all these things by—"

"By steady application and diligent study," said Meade reverently. She admired thorough work of all kinds.

By now it was nearly dark, the lightning bugs were out, and the dew had begun to come down. "Thank you so much for the education you have given us," said Hilma. "You have distinguished our last Thursday in May." It was difficult to walk through the tall ferns, and Hilma and Meade staggered along with their chairs. Lewis walked a little ahead of them with easy, practiced strides. It had not occurred to him to offer to help with the chairs, but Hilma and Meade didn't notice. On the way to the road he pointed out several nesting trees, marked by the apron of white sap on their trunks, and just as they reached the car they caught sight of a tiny bird darting into one of the holes.

"I feel as if I have been blessed," said Hilma. "Thank you so much, Mr. Lewis." She dragged his hand away from the binoculars and shook it warmly.

* * *

"You already know Gawain, and these are our friends Lucy and Ethel," Hilma said to Lewis, with a simplicity that belied the difficulties that had gone into compiling this guest list. Meade had wanted to invite Roger; "I can't imagine such a gathering without Roger," she had said.

"But if we have Roger, then we can't have Ethel," said Hilma, "and if Gawain has Roger to listen to him, there will be nothing but talk of fire."

So in the end they had settled on Gawain, Ethel, and Lucy. "Gawain will make him feel at home, Ethel will entertain him with flash and style, and Lucy will make everything go smoothly." The party was outside, at Hilma's house— "We will hope that the angel's-trumpet will open"—and the food was all summer food: cucumber soup, sliced tomatoes, a Vidalia onion pie, and a triumphant gumbo Lucy had made out of the first crop of a new nematode-resistant okra.

Lewis stood stiff and uneasy in the shade of the crape myrtle, looking unnaturally clean. His neatly parted hair still retained the grooves of the comb teeth, and sharp folds in his shirt stood out like fins in odd places. On his chest a smooth, flat rectangle showed the position of the piece of cardboard that had been slipped out minutes earlier.

"New clothes?" Ethel asked, and she laughed at him. Lewis fumbled at his chest, missing the binoculars, and stepped into the Nicotiana.

"We found him in the woods," Hilma said to Lucy. "We had been sitting there for three Thursdays, doing nothing more interesting than looking for ticks, and there he was. He told us about his study, and then, as if by magic, one of the birds flew by, right into its nest cavity. We heard its little squeak."

Ethel pulled two chairs up to the edge of the garden. "We are all people here, Lewis," she said. She was still laughing. "You are one too."

"He's a fine old-fashioned naturalist as well as a good scientist," said Gawain, "with an ability to see beyond isolated details to the great ecological processes at work."

Ethel sat down on the edge of her chair and leaned forward intently. She had the tiniest kneecaps he had ever seen on a normal-sized person, each one no bigger than a fifty-cent piece, and her shiny brown hair slid against itself like feathers on a bird. "We are supposed to talk to each other, Lewis," she said. "I say something to you. Then it's your turn."

The night flowers began to open, and there was a mingling of the clean smell of the moonflower, the jasminelike Nicotiana, and the odd musky fragrance of the Datura, just now beginning to unfurl. It was a pleasant evening to be outside, eating the first Vidalia onions of the year. Lucy, Meade, Hilma, and Gawain sat under the moonflower trellis talking about nematodes, woodpeckers, fire, and this remarkable new friendship.

"I felt almost like Joan of Arc," said Hilma, "and he was the archangel Michael striding up to us through the green."

"The diminished population of red-cockaded woodpeckers is just one example of the eradication of fire-dependent ecosystems by the exclusion of fire—his work is making that clear," said Gawain.

"He needs to watch out for Ethel," said Lucy, and they all peered around the moonflowers into the garden.

"Oh," said Hilma.

"Oh, Ethel!" said Meade.

"Well, time for me to go home," said Gawain.

"That nice fan man, Jim Wade," said Hilma. "So pleasant and cheerful. Why doesn't Ethel . . ."

"Because she likes to do the choosing," said Lucy.

"I am reminded of mating insects," said Meade.

In the garden Ethel held a branch of angel's-trumpet aside and whispered something in Lewis's ear, then she stepped back, laughing. "Now," she said, "your turn."

"That Ethel!" snapped Meade, slapping a pair of yellow rubber gloves against the edge of the sink. "Carrying on like that before our very eyes in a bed of poisonous plants."

"And what will happen to the poor man now?" Hilma sighed. "He doesn't have Roger's strength."

"I told you we should have invited Roger," said Meade, thrusting her hands into the rubber gloves. "Then what a nice party it would have been, Roger and

Lewis and Gawain discussing the influence of fire on the lives of plants and animals like civilized people."

"Well," said Hilma, trying to look on the bright side, "the garden was lovely, the food was good, and it's always a pleasure to see Lucy."

"I blame it all on the garden," said Meade. "I have never trusted Datura."

"I thought you said sex was best when you weren't having it," said Lucy.

"But I have to check now and then to make sure I'm still right," said Ethel. She had spent the day with Lewis in the woodpecker woods and she was looking for ticks. So far she had found four. "It was an interesting encounter," she said. "He's so delightfully strange. He knows more about those birds than he knows about himself."

"Meade says you remind her of a mating insect," said Lucy.

"Ha," said Ethel. "Good old Meade. Probably a mantis. No, I always leave them alive, Lucy."

"Barely," said Lucy, remembering the Irish Potato Famine.

"He'll get over it," said Ethel. "They always do."

It was late at night and he couldn't make the distances work out. He kept losing count and having to begin again. Was this the sickness of love or was it the mothballs in the bird skins making him feel slightly nauseated and dizzy? "It was nice," she had said. "I enjoyed it. And now I'm going home to my house and you must go home to yours." They were standing at the edge of the woods. On one side, I-10 stretched all the way to California, and on the other side lay a thousand acres of virgin longleaf with five colonies of maybe the last red-cockaded woodpeckers that would live on earth.

"You have to understand," she said, as the cars roared by, "I like a kind of fly-by-night love life. Here today, gone tomorrow." But he did not understand. All he could think of were the thousands of migrating birds that were killed every night when they flew into the guy wires of TV towers.

"There is no hope of recovering the bodies," said Meade, "in all that muck, so the mourners are tossing flowers into the swamp." A small plane had crashed in the middle of the Okefenokee Swamp, and television screens were filled with the sad faces of announcers talking about "human remains." Meade had been taken with the idea of tossing flowers into the swamp.

"Maybe that's what we should do for Lewis," she said.

"It's not as bad as that," said Lucy reasonably. "He was not strapped into his seat, hurtling helplessly through the night sky with one engine burned out."

"Ethel is a good person, really, at heart—good company, an excellent teacher, a good gardener—she learned that from Roger. She just doesn't have tender feelings for the men she knows," said Hilma.

"She doesn't like the constrictions of love," said Lucy.

"Then why does she keep breaking the hearts of these nice men? The song writer from Nashville; poor Jim Wade, the fan man, always so eager for news of Ethel when he sees me; and now Lewis."

"Sex," said Lucy.

"Oh," said Hilma.

"No body parts bigger than an elbow have been found," said Meade.

It was June, but Hilma and Meade were reluctant to give up their May adventures, and they had invited Lewis to present a little program on the life and habits of the red-cockaded woodpecker. But Meade fidgeted in her chair and Hilma felt her mind begin to wander. In May he had come striding out of the green like an angel, with science, the new bracken fern, and all the promise of summer on his side. But now, in her living room, standing beside the portable chalkboard she had dragged down from the attic, he seemed like nothing more than an ordinary man. Hilma was irritated by the way he kept erasing his little sketches with the heel of his hand, leaving damp smudges on the chalkboard so that the blurred lines of a previous diagram showed through his current drawing, muddling his points. Lewis too seemed edgy and dispirited. He kept glancing furtively out into the garden, as if he expected to see Ethel step out of the bed of Datura in her little flowered dress. But no one could stand to be outside in this heat. In the white garden the blooms from the night before were drooping and spent. The Nicotiana hung in slimy wads from its stems, and the petals of the Datura sagged, battered and bruised by the wings of the hummingbird moths.

6. 1914 GENERAL ELECTRIC FAN WITH COLLAR OSCILLATOR

The dog flopped down on the floor, and one ear and a limp black lip spread out along the linoleum. "Don't put your chair down on that dog's ear," said Ethel, but there was a yelp and a cry and the boy leaped up and the chair fell over backward and the dog scrambled to his feet and walked around in little circles looking embarrassed and ashamed.

"I'm sorry, Bud, I'm so sorry, I didn't mean to," Andy said, hugging the old dog.

"Don't worry about that old dog," said Eula. "He'll just find him another cool spot. Andy, Bud, get out of my way, I'm coming through with something hot." And the old dog wandered across the room and lay down in the doorway, looking out with tired, sad eyes at Eula, Ethel, Tom, and Tom's son Andy, who had come all the way from California to spend the summer with his daddy.

"That is one sorry dog," said Tom.

"He's not a sorry dog," said Andy. "He's a good dog—" and then across the room to the dog, "aren't you, Bud?" The dog whacked the floor once with his tail in acknowledgment and crossed his front feet.

"Well," said Eula, "you spend enough time with a dog, you come to love him anyway. It don't matter if he is sorry."

"The money you have poured into that sorry dog," said Tom, "rabies shots, heartworm treatment, worms."

"He's not a sorry dog," said Andy, and his voice rose shrilly. "He's a good dog!"

"I want Andy to come with Jim Wade and me on a fan trip," said Ethel, "up near Abbeville. He needs some parts—blades, a grill. He's trying to put together a—"

"Goddamned sorry dog," said Tom.

"Tom," said Eula, holding on to the edge of the table with both hands.

"You should have left him down at the dump where you found him," said Tom.

"Tom," said Eula. But it was too late. Andy jumped up from the table and ran out of the room. They heard a screen door slam.

Tom began viciously poking food around on his plate. "That's his mama," he said. "His mama has done that to him. And what am I supposed to do about it? I spend, what, three months a year with him?"

"Tom, he's just a little boy," said Eula.

But Tom stabbed a potato with his fork and began gesturing with it. "I send her all this money," he said, "and she raises him up to be like that. He don't like to hunt because he can't stand the sight of blood, he don't like to fish because he can't stand to touch something slimy, he can't go out in the woods because he's allergic to poison ivy. So what's he going to do all summer but mope around in this house full of women and sorry dogs eating up my food and painting moss and buttermilk on flowerpots. Hell, everybody's allergic to poison ivy!"

"Tom, you're scaring us to death with that potato," said Ethel. "Either eat it or put it down. Andy and I are riding up to Abbeville with Jim Wade this weekend. He's looking for electric fans."

"Women, sorry dogs, and nuts," said Tom.

MAKE YOUR OWN MOSSY FLOWERPOTS! the directions said. THEY MAKE GREAT GIFTS FOR YOUR GARDENING FRIENDS!

"But I don't have any gardening friends," said Andy, peering down into the moss and buttermilk slurry in the bucket. "Pew." The mixture had been marinating in the sun for two days.

"Honey," said Ethel, "you go home to California with these mossy flowerpots, gardening friends will come flocking. They'll line the streets. They'll come out of the cracks in the walls at night. Brush it on thick, Buddy Man. Woo, don't you love something that smells that bad!"

Andy sat with his elbows on his knees, moss and buttermilk dribbling off the paintbrush onto the steps. "Everybody I love is divorced," he said. "You and Roger, Mama and Daddy."

"Your granny's not divorced," said Ethel. "Your great-aunt Louise is not divorced."

"But Granddaddy was killed by a tractor. And Louise is crazy, that's worse."

"Look on the bright side," said Eula.

"That's what I always do." And she put her bowl of cucumbers down in her lap and recited:

The flowers must be buried in
  darkness
Before they can bud and bloom,
And the sweetest, warmest sunshine
Comes after the storm and gloom.

"But sometimes there can't be a bright side, right, Buddy?" said Ethel, swabbing drools of green buttermilk off the steps. "All your relatives are divorced, dead, or crazy. You put a chair down on your dog's ear, your mama's a thousand miles away, and your daddy is hateful and mean. What's bright about that, Aunt Eula?"

"That dog's ear ain't hurt," said Eula. "That dog's ear is just fine. Can you stay for supper, Ethel? Beans, corn, tomatoes, a little piece of ham, and these pickles. You could cheer us up."

"Please, Ethel," said Andy.

"Can't, Buddy," said Ethel.

"I'm sorry Ethel couldn't stay to supper," said Eula. "I think these bread-and-butter pickles turned out good this time. Crunchy, that's the lime."

"Ethel!" said Tom. "Only one reason why Ethel couldn't stay to supper. Who is it this time—the woodpecker expert, the Yankee boatbuilder, the songwriter from Nashville, or that nut Jim Wade, the fan man. She don't care. Just so he's got breath and britches."

"Don't start that, Tom," said Eula.

"I don't get it," said Tom. "She had a good man—she had Roger for Chrisake, God's gift to women! I just don't get it."

"Tom," said Eula.

"Promiscuous, is what she is," said Tom.

"She's not!" said Andy, jumping up. "No she's not!" and they heard the screen door slam.

"Jesus!" said Tom. "The dog ain't sorry, Ethel ain't promiscuous, I guess the sun don't rise in the east, I been wrong all my life. Jesus! All I'm doing is telling the truth!"

"Sometimes you don't need to tell the truth, Tom," said Eula. "Sometimes you just need to let the truth alone." But Tom shoved his chair back, the screen door slammed again, and out in the yard the truck engine roared.

Even this late at night it was still hot. Andy sat on the steps in the dark, poking at the scummy pots with a stick. The buttermilk was supposed to promote the growth of the moss, which would then coat the pots with a lush, soft green. But so far there was just the black scum, now beginning to mildew. The whole porch smelled like rotten buttermilk.

"It's the heat that makes him that way, Buddy," Eula said. "Out in the woods all day, in that blistering heat, it boils all his bad thoughts to the surface. Heat makes people mean. You go off with Ethel and Jim Wade tomorrow, maybe we'll get a rain, cool us off, and when you come back there'll be a change. Every cloud has a silver lining!" she said cheerfully.

But later, as she washed the dishes in the kitchen, she couldn't help but notice that a little pile of bread-and-butter pickles had been left on every plate.

"You may not believe it," said Jim Wade, "but summer is the best time to pick up old fans." He was driving his big red van, hunched earnestly over the steering wheel. "People get desperate in this heat, they think they'll be better off with that new model fan from Wal-Mart, a grumbling grandson puts in a window air conditioner for Granny, and the fine old fans end up at the junk stores and flea markets and yard sales."

Ethel was in the front seat reading the map. Andy was sitting in the back surrounded by fans and parts of fans: a tangle of guards, a stepped base and a bundle of rusty struts, a Gilbert Polar Cub with no motor, and a twelve-inch General Electric with an open S-guard and steel blades. It was hot and dry. The grass beside the road was shriveled and silvery from drought, and in the fields irrigation rigs marched majestically across acres of corn and peanuts, spewing fountains of water into the air.

"That's how I got my Cool Spot. Mr. Martin put a window air conditioner in for an old lady over in Colquitt County, and there it was the next day out at Farr Road Flea Market. Just needed a little blade adjustment, that's why it was running ragged. In August the old lady died of a stroke sitting right in front of that 5000-Btu air conditioner. She would have been alive today if she'd kept that Cool Spot—it's a gentler cool."

"Heat makes people mean," said Andy.

"Heat can kill you," said Jim Wade. "You'd be surprised at how many fans I've acquired through deaths."

"No, we wouldn't," said Ethel, "would we, Buddy? Nothing would surprise Buddy and me."

The first thing they noticed about the Kountry Kitchen Restaurant and Motel was the pigs, dozens of jigsawed plywood pigs wearing little painted-on outfits—pants, checked shirts, overalls, and ruffled skirts. A sharp stake was nailed to the back of each pig and driven into the dry, hard ground, so that the pigs appeared to float in the air, buoyed up by heat, their dainty, pointed feet hovering just above the parched grass. On shelves inside the restaurant were more pigs—painted ceramic pigs, tiny pigs made out of pecans, and jars of "pickled" pigs made out of panty hose. The walls of the restaurant were covered with incongruous groupings of old tools—a crosscut saw, an egg beater, an adze, an iron, a pair of butter paddles, a tool for crimping sheet metal, a colander, a milk pitcher, and a couple of saws with scroll-cut handles. The waitress set a dish of pickles down on the table. "Sweet or un?" she said.

"Look, Jim Wade," said Andy, "there's a fan." It sat on a shelf over the kitchen door between a butter churn and a kerosene lantern—a twelve-inch General Electric desk fan with four brass blades and an all-brass guard. For just a minute Jim Wade stared without moving. Then he put his hands on his knees and blew out a little puff of air. He got up, walked over to the doorway, and stood, looking up at the fan, his hands clasped behind his back. The waitress set three glasses of iced tea on the table, pulled out her pad, and licked her pencil. Then she looked over at Jim Wade and sighed. "Is he gon' eat?" she asked.

With a slow, studied saunter Jim Wade made his way back to the table. He settled himself gently into his chair and lounged back. He picked up the menu and flicked it casually aside. His fingers were trembling. The waitress eyed him suspiciously, took a step back, and asked, "What do you want to eat?"

Jim Wade stretched out his legs and let out a long breath. "How much for that fan?" he asked.

"Oh," said the waitress with relief. "This stuff ain't for sale. It's the decor."

"Decor!" said Jim Wade, and he shoved himself up out of his chair with both hands. The dish of pickles slid to the edge of the table. "Decor! Woman, that is a 1914 GE 940566 with a collar oscillator!"

The waitress thrust her pencil behind her ear and snapped her pad against the palm of her hand. "Don't you get rough with me, mister," she said. "You got a problem with the decor, you talk to Mr. Loomis out at the pit."

"No sir, that stuff ain't for sale," said Mr. Loomis. Smoke and flames shot up as he swabbed grease off slabs of meat with a mop. "That's the atmosphere, the country charm."

"Country charm!" wailed Jim Wade, staggering around the piles of firewood. "Atmosphere!" He picked up a piece of hickory wood and threw it back down. "Man, GE only made that collar oscillator one year—1914!" A thick-shouldered red bulldog crouching under a pickup truck watched warily with squinny eyes as Mr. Loomis dragged a pork shoulder from a

Styrofoam cooler and hurled it onto the grill.

"Jim Wade," said Ethel.

With a practiced swing and a smooth toss Mr. Loomis fed another piece of wood to the fire. He reached in with a poker and shifted things around, settling the new wood in among the coals.

"It ain't for sale," he said.

"How about a trade then?" said Jim Wade. "I've got a fan with me right now, a twelve-inch GE, 1922, open S-guard, steel blades, to the untrained eye indistinguishable from the 940566—slip yours out, slip mine in. Your customers would never notice."

Mr. Loomis's eyes were red from the smoke. His short blue T-shirt was stuck to his back in dark blue splotches. His forearms were streaked with black, and his face glistened with soot and sweat.

"Jim Wade," said Andy.

"I'll pay the difference!" said Jim Wade.

Mr. Loomis slowly straightened up and turned to Jim Wade, balancing the poker lightly in one hand. He took a step away from the pit.

"Mister," he said, and just then the dog, in a slinking crouch, shot out from under the truck and snatched at a side of ribs. Without looking around, Mr. Loomis picked up a chunk of firewood and threw it with a neat, snapping toss. It hit the dog hard, square on the side of the head, and knocked him flat. He lay on his side among the pieces of firewood, without making a sound, his feet twitching.

"It ain't for sale," Mr. Loomis said.

Back in the restaurant Jim Wade sat as tight as a knot, his back to the fan, chewing up cinnamon-flavored toothpicks and staring out the window at the sun setting on the plywood pigs. Ethel ate a pickle, but no one touched the ribs and coleslaw. From a back booth the surly waitress glared at them with a cigarette clamped between her lips. Andy kept staring at the pigs on the bathroom doors. One of the pigs had long eyelashes and was wearing a dress with pink polka dots and a bow; on the other door a stern-faced pig dressed in blue overalls was holding a pitchfork.

"Heat makes people mean," said Andy.

The window was higher than he expected. When he had unlocked it from inside the bathroom, the sill had only come up to his waist, but from out here on the ground it was over his head. He had to make a rickety tower of pigs to reach it, and he scuffed up his knees and scraped his elbows scrambling in. Inside, it was dark. The air-conditioning had been turned off and the air was heavy with the smell of cigarettes, vinegar, Pine Sol, and smoked meat. Two phrases kept going through his head, and he chanted them under his breath—"Fans acquired through death" and "It ain't for sale."

In the morning it was drizzling rain. It felt almost cold. Ethel stood at the window of the motel room and looked out at the herd of plywood pigs hovering above the mud in the rain with their cheerful painted-on faces and their silly clothes. "I don't care if I never see another jigsawed pig as long as I live," she said. Andy stood on the sidewalk, watching the diners with their umbrellas and raincoats scurrying in and out of the Kountry Kitchen Restaurant. And Jim Wade stood in the rain at the back door of his van, holding on to the edge of the roof with both hands and staring in at the brass blades of the General Electric 940566.

No one felt like eating breakfast at the Kountry Kitchen and they got home before noon. "Beans, corn, tomatoes, and pickles," said Eula, but Jim Wade said he didn't think he'd better stay for lunch. Andy sat down on the floor and gathered as much of the dog as would fit into his lap and hugged him and hugged him, crooning, "Good dog, good dog," while Ethel told the story of the man and his barbecue and his bulldog and his 1914 GE fan with the rare oscillator.

"I know that like to killed Jim Wade," said Tom, "not getting that fan. No wonder he didn't want to talk about it."

"Good dog," said Andy. "Good dog."

"That fan sitting on a shelf, just for looks, not doing anybody any good," said Tom. "You know, if it had been me, I'd of stole that fan."

Then from out on the porch Ethel called, "Mossy pots!" and sure enough, on the moldy sides of the pots they could see little tendrils of green twining through the black scum.

7. BIRDING

"Prothonotary," said Roger, peering through the binoculars.

"Eeenh," she said. It was a sound she made, indicating uncertainty or polite disagreement. In the three hours they had been together on this bird-watching expedition, she had made that sound twice. Roger was uneasy. He handed her the binoculars.

"Pine warbler," she said. Marsh birds were her specialty, but because of the nature of her art she would be uncomfortable with a misidentified warbler. She did not know that Roger was in love with her, that he had been smitten ever since the day she had left a Hamilton Beach electric blender at the dump. She did not know that he had spent hours studying her paintings at the gallery downtown, admiring the sunlight on the black water, the glistening lily pads, the birds visible only in glimpses, almost hidden in reeds and grasses. She did not know how very much he admired the spare, straightforward titles she gave her pictures— *Nesting Coot, Common Gallinules, Pied-billed Grebe and Young.* She did not know that he had been stalking her in a civilized way for weeks, working up from the startling "Have a nice day" at an accidental meeting at the Dumpster to this bird-watching expedition in a wildlife refuge on a barrier island off the coast. She did not know that simply reading Peterson's description of her birds, family Rallidae, ". . . rather hen-shaped marsh birds of secretive habits and mysterious voices," made him weak and shaky.

So it had not been easy for Roger, standing in the litter of the dump on that summer day a week ago, a swarm of sulfur butterflies congregating on a puddle of drool from the Dumpster and a spent "easy glide" tampon applicator at his heel, it had not been easy for him to draw a breath and say, "Have you ever seen the marsh birds in Little Tired Slough out on Cathead Island? Because of my plant work I have a permit, and I could take you there."

And yet how easy it had been for her to heft her bag of garbage up over the lip of the Dumpster and turn to him as the swarm of sulfur butterflies rose up and surrounded her in a winkling yellow column, how very easy it had been for her to lift her hands, palms up into the butterflies, smile, and say, "Might we see rails there?"

On the ferry to Cathead Island they had sat side by side between canvas bags and ice chests, listening to a lively, talkative woman describe with animated gestures a study she was conducting on the life cycle of the oyster. Roger couldn't stop watching her dry-looking, rather gray tongue, which wagged restlessly back and forth in her open mouth during pauses as if it were feeling around for the next phrase. Della sat very still, her hands cupped in her lap. Every now and then, with a practiced sweep she would lift her binoculars to her eyes, follow a gliding bird for a minute, then lower the binoculars and curl her hands back in her lap. Nothing but pelicans and gulls. What have I done, Roger thought, and then she leaned over to him and whispered, "Like the tongue of a bored parrot." Roger longed to hug her, but he could only close his eyes and nod emphatically.

Since that shining moment, however, he had misidentified a warbler, and in their three hours of walking along the little sandy trails through the marshes and scrub, they had seen nothing more exciting than a kingfisher, an osprey, an anhinga, and some herons. She kept poking things at the edge of the marsh and making minute examinations of bits of dung.

"Otter," she said, delicately picking around in it with two sticks. Roger stood and looked out toward the gulf, thinking of the birds he would will to this marsh for her: the big pink and green waders— a pair of roseate spoonbills with blood-red drips on their shoulders, American flamingos, a flock of scarlet ibises blown north of their range by a hurricane. Then a scattering of little jewel-like birds—painted buntings, golden-crowned kinglets, blue grosbeaks, and vermilion flycatchers. She put down the two sticks and stood up.

"They've been eating fiddler crabs," she said.

In the midafternoon they sat down to rest on a plank bridge at the marshy edge of a little pine woods. The trees had been turpentined in the 1920s, and they were stunted and brushy-topped, with old chevron-shaped scars making something like faces on their trunks. The hot sun brought out the droughty, sharp smells of a forest that has lived a hard life—oozing pine sap, baking lichens, and dry sand. From the woods they could hear the raucous laughter of pileated woodpeckers, and from the marsh the herons gave out their hoarse croaks. Roger watched her feet dangling over the black water of Little Tired Creek in their battered tan boots and remembered Peterson's picture of a coot's foot, in the corner of a page, elegantly enclosed in a circle, the ankle relaxed, the toes swagging gracefully. "Lobed foot of Coot," the caption read.

Then she said, "Feet!" and she pointed. "There's a snowy egret; I have nightmares about those yellow feet," she said urgently, handing Roger the binoculars. Sure enough, at the end of the bird's gleaming black legs were a pair of startling yellow feet.

"You have nightmares about the feet of snowy egrets?" said Roger, lowering the binoculars. In an access of love, he began unpacking food and spreading it out on the bridge. Hard-boiled eggs, bread, cheese, pickles, Penrose sausages, jalapeño peppers, apples, and an alligator pear. "What do the feet do in your dreams?" he asked. He started handing her bits of food, which she ate solemnly, still looking at the edge of the marsh.

"Usually they just stand there," she said. "But sometimes one foot will pick up and begin to step. That's what makes it a nightmare instead of just a dream." Then she recited, " 'When feeding, rushes about, shuffling feet to stir up food.' That's what it says in Peterson's." She looked at Roger with her steady and earnest gaze. "Just think about it, Roger."

But for the rest of the afternoon all Roger could think about was how much he wanted to protect this peculiar and delicate woman from every harm, to keep her safe and well fed, and to rid her dreams forever of yellow, shuffling feet. The sun was dipping down below the tops of the trees as they headed back through the little woods to the ferry dock. She didn't talk, but now and then she would lift the binoculars to her eyes without breaking her stride and whisper the names of birds on an intake of breath: "Coot," "Grebe," "Sandpipers— Snowy, eeehn, no—" and she stopped. "Ha! immature little blue." In the distance, across the last stretch of marsh, Roger could see the ferry dock. The water had turned from its midday aqua and indigo to a dark greasy gray. "I'll just take one last look," she said, and she left the little sandy path and carefully stepped along a narrow trail through the marsh grass. She moved slowly, stopping and starting like a snake sneaking up on a rat. At the edge of a little inlet she squatted down and lifted the binoculars, her elbows propped on her knees. On the other side of the water, a little dark shape rustled in the grass and was gone.

Della straightened up wearily, like an old fighter might stretch at the end of a great fight. She straightened her legs with her hands on her knees, then she straightened her back, then she straightened her shoulders. She turned and made her careful way out of the marsh. "Whoo!" she said, and she smiled. She stood in front of Roger and put one hand on his chest, fingers spread, and looked at him at arm's length. "A black rail," she said. "Number 397."

The ride back to the mainland was peaceful. The parrot-tongued woman was quiet, wearied by her day's study of the lives of oysters, and Della had the beatific look of a satisfied birder. The boat captain set the autopilot and sat down in an aluminum chair with his book. The engine droned.

Della turned to Roger. "I enjoy chickens," she said.

But Roger was not surprised. She didn't smile, and he didn't expect her to. She was a serious woman, with her mind on birds.

"Not White Leghorns, though," she said.

"No," said Roger slowly. "Certainly not

White Leghorns." He squinted thoughtfully. "I would think Golden Sebrights."

"Yes," she said, nodding emphatically.
"And Silver-laced Wyandottes."

"Buff Orpingtons," said Roger.

"Dominiques," she said, beginning to
smile.

"Punkin Holses," said Roger, "Laken-
velders, and Salmon Favorolles."

Then she laughed out loud and
hugged him tight with both arms. She
smelled like pine trees and lichens and
hot sand. How odd, thought Roger, that
after all, this is what it took—not a flock
of scarlet ibises or golden-crowned
kinglets, but just the names of chickens,
hovering in the air like the sulfur butterflies at the dump.

8. FOUR CHICKENS

"And the plane burst into flames on the runway," Della mumbled under her breath. It was something she always recited at takeoff and landing, the most dangerous parts of airplane flight, she had read. Sometimes she would only say part of the sentence: ". . . into flames . . ." or even just "And the plane . . ." But this time she felt need of the whole thing, and even said it a second time, out loud, looking her seatmate square in the eyes. "And the plane burst into flames on the runway."

But he quickly turned away, stuffing his newspaper into the seat pocket in front of him. Then there was a gentle thump, a kindly voice warned them that items may have shifted during flight, and suddenly they were all on their feet, gathering packages and stirring up the smells of nervous, crowded people.

Della had been in airports and on airplanes all day, making her way up the continent to the prestigious Birds in Art exhibit in Wausau, Wisconsin, where a painting of hers had been accepted. In fact, on this early fall day the air was filled with bird artists: from Sweden, Master Wildlife Artist Lars Jonsson flew in with a mysterious and fantastical icescape featuring six king eiders in the foreground; from Belgium, Carl Brenders flew in with a hyperrealistic gouache and watercolor of a rufous-sided towhee reflected in the rearview mirror of a Harley-Davidson motorcycle; and from Connecticut, Roger Tory Peterson flew in with a field-guide plate of flycatchers in profile, dutifully displaying their field marks. There were the old-fashioned gentlemen/naturalist artists and their Audubonesque bird portraits, there were the hot-blooded activist artists with their shocking pictures of dead birds and human filth. There were artists with tiny, precise watercolors of songbirds, and artists with life-size carvings of swooping fish eagles and mantling hawks.

But even in all this variety Della was uneasy, and as she made her way through the airport she imagined a steady sibilance trailing behind her, one word spitting itself out of every sentence:

At Gate B-22: *"Chickens!"*

On the moving sidewalk: "She has painted *chickens!*"

At the baggage carousel: *"Imagine! Chickens!"*

"You have submitted a picture of chickens to Birds in Art?" Lou, the gallery owner back home, had said, standing back and looking at it.

"Dominiques," said Della. "An old utility breed."

"To the most important wildlife art show in the world, you have submitted chickens?"

"They are considered endangered by the American Livestock Breeds Conservancy," said Della.

"Endangered chickens!" Lou said, and he flipped through the Birds in Art catalog, pausing pointedly at the John Felsing oil of roseate spoonbills in a south Florida sunset and the Guy Coheleach African fish eagle flying in front of Victoria Falls, its wings dramatically poised on the downstroke.

"Chickens!" Lou stepped back and held out his arms, palms up, to the picture of the two Dominiques scratching in the dirt. "Della! Landsdowne will be there! Robert Bateman will be there! Hartsfield! Hartsfield himself could see this!"

But it was too late; a week later the letter came in the mail:

Dear Ms. Robinson:
We are happy to announce ...

"I'm thinking about your reputation as a serious wildlife painter, Della," Lou said. They were having lunch together "to celebrate," Della had said.

"Chickens." Lou began tearing his roll into bite-size pieces and smearing butter on them with slashing strokes. "Your title is *Chickens,* but what are you really telling the viewer with this painting, Della? Is it about confinement? Man's dominance over avian life? Or is it simply a portrait of light? Which would be *fine.*" He laid down his knife and the last bit of bread, crossed his arms on the edge of the table, and leaned across his plate earnestly. "But in the changing world of wildlife art you must have the courage of your convictions. You must have convictions, Della. . . . Do you?" He bit sharply into a piece of bread, cleaving it cleanly in two. It was almost a snap.

"It's just a picture of chickens, Lou," Della said bravely.

And as *Chickens* the painting had been crated up and shipped to Wisconsin, where it was carefully hung on a white wall in a glow of even light. "Chickens" had been crisply printed on a creamy card enclosed in a plastic sheath below the picture.

"Chickens!" a woman in a sable coat snorted, reading the title, and leaned in for a closer look. "I just don't know where wildlife art is headed," she said to her husband, a bland, tall man with rimless glasses and an ascot, and together they glided on.

That night, at a Birds in Art fete hosted by museum patrons after the Friday evening private showing, Della was seated beside Bruce Coulton, a painter of scenes of conquest and lavish sexual display in equatorial Africa. He had just stopped smoking, and jet lag and the longing for nicotine made him a trying companion.

"Mr. Coulton has torn himself away from his rain forest to honor us here with those magnificent flamingos," announced their hostess, who had just donated a collection of Victorian crystal bird nests to the museum. "We do appreciate your leaving your exciting life and your *work,* which must be so consuming, Mr. Coulton. And you"—she peered around the Asian lilies to see Della's name tag— "yours is the . . ."

"Chickens," said Della.

"Oh yes, the chickens," cried the hostess, throwing up her hands. "I love your wonderful chickens!" She laid her hand on Bruce Coulton's arm and whispered, "I suppose we must paint what we know, and make the best of it, must we not, Mr. Coulton!"

Bruce Coulton started in his seat and sucked in air between his teeth. But smoking was not allowed in this restored

Georgian mansion, and after coffee and dessert, Della, seeking air, found him standing in the middle of a little sculpture garden lighting a cigarette with trembling fingers. He breathed in deeply, eyes closed, the cigarette cupped in his palm as if he expected it to be snatched away from him. The cold, the dark, the glowing cigarette, and the eerie modern sculptures of tortured-looking animals reclining on pads of white gravel gave a theatrical, almost sinister feel to the moment, and when Bruce Coulton barked out, "Is Hartsfield here?" Della started.

"He always comes the second day, for the opening," she said.

"A grand entrance," he said, squinting his eyes and sucking on his cigarette. "Swooping down on us all in that gray cape."

"It would be a grand entrance no matter when he came," said Della.

Hartsfield had not painted since the winter day ten years ago when he had fallen out of a small boat while sighting an Atlantic puffin off the coast of Maine. But every year he made an appearance at the Birds in Art exhibit, moving silently through the throng on the arm of his companion, his cashmere cape slipping off his gaunt shoulders. The crowd would part at his approach, making way for the great man, and the museum director would stop him at each picture with a gentle tug, whispering the name of the artist and the title of the work. He never commented, but sometimes he would fold himself over at the waist, peer at one corner of a painting, and say "Hmmm" before moving on.

"I don't know why he bothers to come," said Bruce Coulton, viciously stubbing out his cigarette in the gravel. "His mind is gone, his work is passé, he drools, and he's blind as a bat." He paused and glared at the sculpture, a smooth, almost featureless pair of panthers reclining languidly on their bed of gravel, their stubby, undifferentiated paws not quite settling down. "Jesus! They look like victims of thalidomide." He poked at one of the cats with his toe. "Where are we headed in this genre?" he growled, and then he stalked off toward the light, leaving Della with the white panthers and the last wisps of smoke, feeling uneasy. It was the second time today that that question had been addressed to her, more or less rhetorically. She thought about Hartsfield's magnificent body of work in the museum's permanent collection: mantling hawks draped in their own wings, eider ducks in an Arctic mist, an imperial eagle and its prey. Then she thought about her own painting of the two Dominiques, and how she had struggled and suffered with it through a whole summer. In the end it had come to this—just chickens.

The next day was gray and cold, with a low sky and a forecast of snow. The crowd formed a line in the icy sculpture garden, and slowly the galleries filled. The excellent lighting in the museum made it seem as if the people themselves were on display—their hair shone, their faces glowed, and their jewelry flashed and glinted. They flowed through the rooms like a viscous liquid, forming little stagnant pools near the works of the most famous artists and babbling with awe and admiration.

At ten o'clock sharp Hartsfield arrived. He paused for a moment in the open doorway to recover his balance after the dangerous work of stepping over the threshold, and a cold wind gusted into the museum.

Hartsfield's clothes draped off the angles of his gaunt old frame like plumage—the gray cape forming itself into long folds like primary feathers, a ruby scarf peeking through mufflers of brown and tan at his throat. His friends gathered around, and art was forgotten as everyone watched Roger Tory Peterson, Robert Bateman, and J. Fenwick Lansdowne greet the great man. No one touched him for fear of upsetting his balance, but one by one they nodded and bowed and smiled and murmured their greetings.

Then the methodical tour began. *"Osprey and Atlantic Salmon,* by Larry Barth. *Sooty Shearwater,* by Charles Greenough Chase. *Purple-crested Loerie,* Dino Paravano,"* the museum director murmured confidentially, and "SOOTY SHEARWATER . . . that's CHASE, CHARLES CHASE," Hartsfield's companion clarified, in a louder voice.

"Mmmm," said Hartsfield, pausing and stooping. "Hmmm."

"Chickens, Della Robinson," said the museum director.

Hartsfield stooped and peered. His lower eyelids had lost their elasticity, and they sagged away from his eyes, giving the illusion that at any moment both eyeballs might roll out of their sockets. Della fought back an urge to cup her two hands helpfully at his cheeks. Slowly Hartsfield reached out and made a trembling, pinching gesture. "Dominickers!" he said in a voice that sounded like a gleeful squawk, and his companion roared, "CHICKENS!"

9. LIBRARY PICNIC

"Smokey Bear is the most destructive animal that ever walked the North American continent," said Gawain. He was sitting in Hilma's kitchen drinking coffee and talking about fire. Three medium-sized bass were twitching in the sink and Hilma was sharpening her long knife. On most days she was happy to clean Gawain's fish and listen to him talk about environmental salvation by fire, but on this day she wanted to talk about Roger and Della, the bird-watcher.

"Nothing wrong with watching birds," said Gawain. "You can learn a lot by watching birds. Take the falcons that used to nest on bluffs of the Wisconsin River in the early 1900s. The bluffs were open then, kept open by natural fire. Now, because of fire suppression, those bluffs are grown up in thickets, and the falcons are gone. They need an open vista, same as our red-cockaded woodpeckers here. You see it everywhere, Hilma, and birds are just one indication of it; we have caused more environmental damage through the exclusion of fire than any other thing we've done."

"But Gawain," said Hilma, "she seems so . . . well, she has such a one-track mind. It's just coots, gallinules, and rails. What about Roger's music? What about his roses? What about his heirloom hot pepper work in New Mexico?"

"Hilma," said Gawain, "I remember the fire Roger had up in that beautiful stand of longleaf pine two years ago, fire creeping along no higher than a man's head, creeping through the young trees, burned every inch of those woods, and, Hilma, I swear to God, not one needle on those trees was browned. And the next fall that woods was twenty-five acres of solid wire grass in full bloom. A man who knows fire that intimately, and uses it that elegantly, you don't need to worry about the love life of a man like that."

Hilma cleaned the fish on the sink drainboard and stealthily tucked away two of the fillets in the back of her refrigerator.

"Fire is nature's finest tool," said Gawain, shoving his coffee saucer back with both thumbs and standing up emphatically. Then he scooped his fish into a plastic bag and was gone, and Hilma was left picking fish scales off the walls and wondering about fire and the tools of love.

That night Meade and Lucy came for supper to eat the fish with lemon and little green onions, and to make plans for the library's fall fund-raising picnic. After a discussion of casseroles and finger food the talk turned to Roger.

"He found her at the dump," said Meade, "a poor little thrown-away forlorn creature. So like Roger to help a person like that, but now she has wormed her way into his affections, and what is he to do?"

"It wasn't exactly like that, Meade," explained Lucy. "They had their first real meeting out on Cathead Island."

"Well, that's no better," said Meade. "All that heat and salt water, even a reasonable man might lose control of his affections in a place like Cathead Island, and then what is he to do when he finds his feet firmly back on the mainland?"

"I am so worried about Roger's work with heirloom peppers," said Hilma.

"If only she had not thrown away that blender," said Meade. "If only she had taken it to the Goodwill like a sensible woman."

"Roger, come up here and get you something to eat," said Eula, spooning food onto a plate with one hand and shoving chairs to the side to make room for one more with her hip. "Tom's gone to Jacksonville to put Andy on the airplane, Louise is back in the back rattling around with a piece of a sign she made me pick up off 98, I've got fifteen squash casseroles for the library, sit down there, Roger, you know I've got plenty. Now what's this everybody's telling me about you taking up with some woman, she's not from around here, they say, a Yankee is she, now that's all right, Roger, don't get me wrong, some of those people are just as nice as they can be, what is she, she stuffs birds, something about birds, Tom told me. We're really happy for you, Roger," and she gave Roger a little hug and sat down at her place to watch him eat. "Ethel's my own flesh and blood, Roger, but . . ." She reached over and squeezed Roger's hand as if she were feeling for lumps in dough. "Now tell me all about it."

"She doesn't stuff birds, Eula," Roger explained, "she paints birds."

"Paints them?" said Eula. "Seems like most birds look pretty colorful already—redbirds, bluebirds, jaybirds—now there's a pretty bird, a jaybird. Of course you've got your drab sparrows in the fall, they could use a little extra color. . . . She paints birds, now that's something new to me—and very interesting."

"She paints pictures of birds, Eula," Roger said. "Mostly marsh birds. She paints the birds and the plants and water around them."

"Oh!" said Eula, covering her face with a napkin. "Pictures of birds! What was I thinking of? Roger get some of this good squash casserole, Lucy told me ten, but I made fifteen. The library will never miss it. Pictures of birds! Well, I declare! Just like Audubon!"

Lucy and Hilma were making cheese straws for the library fund-raising picnic. "You didn't worry when Roger was married to Ethel, Hilma," said Lucy. "Roger actually began his heirloom pepper research in the early years of his marriage. And Ethel certainly never encouraged him in his music." Lucy paused, remembering "little hands that held me tight, just wave good-bye tonight." "And yet he kept picking and fiddling." Lucy screwed down the handle of the cookie press and extruded a row of crimped cheese straws. "And although Ethel is my dear friend, I can't imagine a worse woman for a man to be married to," she added.

"But we were used to Ethel," said Hilma.

"And so will you get used to the bird-watching woman," said Lucy, snapping off a cheese straw with a flick of the wrist. "You will meet her at the library picnic, and she will say something wise or kind, and you will come to like her."

* * *

"You said ten, I made fifteen, but then Roger came for lunch, and I gave one to Gawain, you know how he can get sometimes, so there's thirteen." Eula stood back modestly and wiped her hands on her apron. The casseroles were neatly lined up on the scrubbed kitchen table in desperately miscellaneous containers, everything from dented stainless steel and chipped-up spatterware to the last one, in a porcelain potty with two ears. Lucy wasn't sure how they would fit in with the rather elegant setting, a brand-new "plantation" house lent to the library for this occasion. But she said, "They smell so good, Eula."

"That's the nutmeg," said Eula. "I always add nutmeg to squash casserole, it does a little something. Yes, I will say, I'm pleased with them. Roger was very complimentary, but then I always love to feed Roger. He told me about this little bird-watching woman he met down at the Dumpster, she paints PICTURES of birds, he tells me, like Audubon."

"He's throwing himself away," said Meade. "The finest man I know is putting his heart into the hands of a woman who never held anything more precious than a pair of spyglasses."

"I imagine she puts those spyglasses down now and then," said Lucy, and there was a thoughtful pause.

"She's not from around here, but I'm sure she's a fine woman," said Eula. "I know Roger wouldn't take up with anybody wasn't nice; well, there was Ethel, but Roger was young then. Plus Ethel's not so bad, she's just a hard woman, needs to keep to herself."

"My God, is it a house or a funeral parlor?" gasped Meade. The house was massive, dark red and purple brick, with many glittering windows. But the towering Corinthian columns looked oddly insubstantial, as if they were made out of Styrofoam. Eula dug in one of the flutes with her thumbnail; it did not leave a dent.

Steve, the librarian, looking harried, helped them carry the casseroles around back, where card tables covered with white linen were arranged in a kind of courtyard between two wings of the house. "Wait until you see the inside," he said ominously.

Eula cupped her hands around the

casseroles and fretted that they would be cold, even though Lucy had assured her that they would be reheated before serving. "PICTURES of birds, PICTURES of birds," she kept reminding herself.

Meade stood imperiously on the steps, overseeing all and thinking, He is throwing himself away, and I will be required to look her in the eye and say something pleasant.

And Hilma went to work layering cheese straws on a silver platter and repeating Lucy's words to herself: "You will meet her at the library picnic, and you will like her."

At six o'clock people began to arrive, dressed to the teeth in raw silk and linen and dark fall suits, the women relentlessly cheerful, the men sweating and smiling bravely. They had each paid fifty dollars to eat a bit of chicken, a scoop of squash casserole, a few string beans, and a dish of ice cream, and to get a peek inside this house that had been a-building for over a year now. The courtyard was filled with the chirps, cackles, and squeals of a crowd of people determined to have a good time. And then, at the top of the steps, there was Roger.

"Oh," said Hilma, and cheese straws began slipping dangerously close to the edge of the platter.

Della stood behind him, dressed in white and tan and looking rather drab and solemn.

"Well," sniffed Meade, "she doesn't look like much."

Perhaps because of his years of walking in densely planted fields of tobacco and peanuts, Roger had a graceful way of moving through a crowd, gently slipping between the people as if they were sticky, floppy leaves that he must not bruise. Della followed in his wake less gracefully, her head lowered and her arms stiff at her sides.

She's nervous, thought Lucy. And they were a frightening sight: Hilma, frozen with her platter of cheese straws, looking stricken, Meade drawing herself up regally, and Eula clutching a squash casserole and saying, "Oh, here's Roger! Don't he look just like himself?"

The introductions were awkward and stiff; Hilma couldn't manage to shake hands because of the cheese straws, and Meade, straining to strike the bird theme right away, told Della she looked just like an English sparrow in her white and tan. But unfortunately everyone's mind instantly settled on other aspects of the English sparrow—an introduced bird, not native to North America, often thought of as a "nuisance" species—and there was an uncomfortable pause. Only Roger knew just what to do. He took the squash casserole out of Eula's hands and gave her a hug, he gave Meade a tiny kiss on the cheek, and then he stood with an arm around Hilma's shoulders and talked easily about this house: Eula's son Tom had sawed 6,000 board feet of heart pine for the flooring and wainscoting, the doors were solid mahogany, and the windows had been milled at an old variety works in north Alabama. The house's owner, who had made millions of dollars selling funeral insurance in Atlanta, was something of a sportsman, and Roger had heard that the walls of one room, above Tom's wainscoting, were covered with murals of hunting scenes. Lucy, sensing that Della might be feeling as if she had fallen into a nest of snakes, suggested that they move through the crowd back to the house. "We will give ourselves a tour," she said brightly. "Della can tell us what she thinks of the painting."

"I'm afraid it won't be quite like what I do," said Della feebly.

"I should think not," said Meade in a loud voice. "Coots, gallinules, and rails are hardly sporting birds."

"Although Tom has shot coots," put in Eula. "Kind of a fishy taste to a coot—not as bad as an anhinga though—now that's a nasty bird to eat. We only ate them once. I don't know what you call an anhinga where you come from, but we call them a snakebird," she said to Della.

"I just call them anhingas," Della gasped simply.

Inside the central hall it was dark and cool. The walls were painted a "hunter" green, and the bright new pine wainscoting and flooring had been darkened with a layer of walnut stain. Everywhere was the smell of new wood and plastic and the gleam of high-gloss polyurethane. A few people came and went from the bathrooms upstairs and downstairs, saying "Ooh" and "Aah" and "What a house!" and "Isn't it just beautiful?"

Roger scouted ahead and found the "media room" with the murals, and they all gathered in the doorway and gazed inside.

On the wall behind a giant television an ostentatious dawn was breaking, and all around the room, much larger than life-size ducks and geese were frozen in flight behind computers, fax machines, and telephones. The paint had been ponderously applied, and the birds had a heavy, almost static look. Labrador retriever dogs with thick red tongues splashed in dry-looking water, and huge, square-jawed men in tiny boats on garishly colored lakes and marshes aimed guns at the stationary birds. "SHOOT ME" was the unmistakable theme of the artwork; and where the painter left the theme, the taxidermist took it up and drove it home: sticking out from the mural on metal rods were real ducks and geese that had indeed been shot and were now gathering dust in full flight.

No one said anything for a minute. Then Roger whispered, "Good God," and Eula said, "Just look at them, poor things, all that flying and not getting anywhere."

"They look so—well, dead," said Lucy.

Meade began examining a giant white

and black goose flying over the fax machine, its withered orange feet dangling into the paper tray, its glass eyes gazing desperately at the big-screen television on the south wall. "This bird is NOT in Peterson's!" she declared shrilly.

But Della just leaned her head back against the wall. She touched her forehead gently with her fingertips. Then she looked at Hilma and reached out a trembling hand. She said, "I think . . . I can't . . . Please . . ."

"My dear child," said Hilma, and she took Della firmly by both arms and led her briskly out of the room, down the hall, and out the front door, where Della squatted on the edge of the steps and vomited into the new foundation planting of boxwoods.

On the other side of the house the library patrons began lining up to serve their plates, but Hilma and Della sat together on the steps for a few minutes. Every now and then Della would shudder, put her head in her hands, and say, "Whoo!" and Hilma would pat her gently on the back and say, "There now, my dear!"

10. EARLY MUSIC

Things were not going well with a water-color of three limpkins in a buttonbush, and after an afternoon spent pacing back and forth in front of the painting and eyeing it warily, her two hands clutched in her armpits and her teeth clenched, Della had gone out into her little neglected yard and ferociously snatched up clumps of daisy-type chrysanthemums by the back steps to give to Hilma. But pulled away from their neighbors, the little plants looked scraggly and sparse, unsuitable as a gift for a new friend, Della thought, and with dirt still under her fingernails she had gone over to the university to hear a concert of medieval music played on period instruments. She had thought that she would be soothed by these small sounds, tweaked and puffed from violas and krummhorns like the music of civilized insects, but the next day when she faced the limpkins once again, she imagined that she could still hear the relentless whine of the hurdy-gurdy buzzing in her ears.

She had been working on this picture for so long that she had felt her style shifting as different areas of the painting neared completion, and now that it was almost finished, the sections began to merge ungraciously, with rattling edges. Della felt shaky and uneasy, as if she might never be able to paint again, but would instead live a squashed and stunted life, crippled by odd nervous tics, strange twitches, and repetitive gestures.

"She's peculiar," Meade said to Hilma. "That way she has of walking, as if she's being blown along by a gusty wind and at any moment might veer around and head off in another direction."

They were picking through the tangle of chrysanthemums Hilma had found on her back steps, their roots wrapped in wet newspapers. "Oh, look!" Hilma had said. "My favorites—the pink single ones."

"Bare roots," sniffed Meade, "and in full bloom. They'll never make it."

"They needed thinning," said Hilma, taking up her trowel and the little plants.

"How strange," said Meade, "to leave them here on the steps, without even a note."

"When they bloom next October we will remember this gift," said Hilma.

"If they live," said Meade.

Della did have an unpredictable gait, Hilma noticed, a sort of gawky meandering saunter. She might come unexpectedly to a complete halt, or she might wheel around and walk backward for a few steps, looking intently into the sky at nothing at all. It was a cool fall afternoon and they were taking a walk with Roger in the park and talking about bird identification and the concept of "jizz."

"I love that word," said Roger, " 'a distinct physical attitude totally apart from any specific field mark, essentially an amalgam of shape, posture, and behavior, in some cases more reliable than rote observation of detail.'" He had been admiring the limpkins in Della's troubling painting. "But that's just how limpkins do!" he had boomed encouragingly. "They hobble around on the limbs of trees just like that, looking frail and gimpy."

But it wasn't the posture or the attitude of the birds that worried Della, and well-meaning words of praise just jangled in her head without a purpose and made her wince. "It's not the birds," she said, and she tried to explain about the clashing transitions and the unpleasing contrasts.

"Remember your chickens," said Hilma. "You need to sleep on it, my dear."

But even in her sleep Della breathed in frightened gasps, and in the morning she woke up feeling dense and heavy. All day she felt an urge to keep herself close together, her thumbs curled secretively beneath her clamped fingers and her arms tight at her sides.

In the evening, after the early sunset, she crept to her drawing table for the first time that day and switched on the light.

The dabs of paint she had mixed when she last had a hope that the painting could be salvaged, and the sponges, razor blades, and brushes optimistically lined up in neat rows now seemed like things that a foolish stranger might have left there long ago. Without even looking at the picture, Della took it up from the table, and with a pair of orange-handled scissors she cut it neatly into eight little pieces and stuffed them away deep in the trash basket.

That night she slept a dark and peaceful sleep, and in the morning when she went outside, for the first time that year she heard the thin quavering song of the white-throated sparrow. She stood still for a minute, breathing easily in and out, and suddenly she thought of the concert of medieval music, and she remembered how at the end of each piece the young musicians had looked up at the audience with amazement and delight, as if they themselves could not quite believe that they had actually made music with those little buglike instruments.

11. ASHES

"I don't think this is a very good idea," said Hilma, clutching the edges of the boat. But even though it was her own mother's ashes they were about to sprinkle in the bay, no one listened to her.

"Over there," called Meade, "in sight of that line of trees. She loved those little coastal oaks, didn't she, Hilma?"

"Sasanquas were her favorite tree," said Hilma, but already Ethel had done something with the tiller and a rope she held in one hand, and the little boat was nosing toward a muddy shoal of black muck pocked with fiddler-crab holes and little piles of gray mud.

Ethel had built this sailboat for herself during the summer with the help of a boatwright she had taken up with from Portsmouth, New Hampshire. It was a beautiful little thing, a New Jersey melon seed, with poplar strakes so thin that Ethel could pick the boat up in one hand and the mast and sail in the other and walk to the edge of the water. Hanging in its sling from the ceiling in Ethel's living room, it had looked so beautiful and delicate, like a rose petal, that Hilma had agreed to go along with this wild adventure. But now the boat seemed so very tippy, and the icy water so very black, and the rope that Ethel tugged seemed dangerously tight, and the boat shot through the water with such silent speed that it almost took Hilma's breath away. Plus, for some reason the memories of her mother were flooding back, and suddenly she could almost see her sitting in her chair by the bird window in their old house on just such a fall day as this fifty years ago and saying, "Oh, Hilma, look, the sasanqua is in bloom!"

Ethel was talking about estuaries now, their amazing fecundity, and how 98 percent of all ocean life begins here, so appropriate for sprinkling the ashes of the dead; and Meade was clutching the tin box between her knees and leaning out to one side so that for a second a thin sheet of green water came sliding over the rail. Suddenly Hilma turned loose, held up both hands in the air, and shouted, "Stop!" Ethel instantly turned loose of everything, and amazingly the little boat did stop, and wallowed there among the waves as if it did not have the first notion of forward movement. They both stared back at Hilma, Meade with a look of consternation, Ethel looking concerned, and Hilma felt the hot tears on her cold face and she almost snatched the tin box from Meade. The boat tipped and slued, Meade said, "Good heavens, Hilma, what ails you?" and Hilma covered her face with her skirt in shame, and thought, an eighty-year-old woman sobbing on the high seas.

"Sasanquas were her favorite tree," she said at last, and Meade said, "But sasanquas are such a common, ordinary tree!" But Ethel said kindly, "We'll go back," and she did something with a rope and called out cheerfully, "Duck!" And then the sail swept back across the boat, and suddenly the water was rushing by again and the green land drew closer and closer.

"I was so embarrassed, Roger," said Hilma. "We had driven all that way, and Ethel navigating that little boat so expertly through a stormy sea. Meade was disappointed. Ethel too, although she didn't say so."

"It wasn't a stormy sea," said Roger. "It was a 'light chop.' And both Meade and Ethel loved it, you know they did. It was an adventure."

They were sitting in Hilma's living room with a little fire in the stove, the first of the fall. Roger had brought gifts suited to this season of transition—a bundle of kindling and a bunch of his last roses. This is more like it, thought Hilma. These small comforts—a pot of soup on the stove, the smell of the roses and the kindling, and a dear friend on the sofa wearing wool socks; not that black water and mud riddled with fiddler-crab holes, and Meade scrabbling at the lid of the can with her fingertips, about to fling the ashes of a loved one against that cold, gray sky.

But now Roger was talking about sasanquas. He was remembering the sasanqua in the garden at his old home place, a pink one, very fragrant, and the little seedlings that would come up all around it in the spring. Being at the far end of the garden, it had survived the fire, and now there was a little grove of sasanquas. He made a point of going out to see them in November when they bloomed, and if Hilma would like it, one sunny day they could take her mother's ashes and sprinkle them in the sasanqua grove.

But suddenly, with her soup spoon in her hand and the last bright roses of summer in the middle of the table, Hilma realized why all this talk of sprinkling made her uneasy: there was a comfort, after all these years, in having her mother's ashes with her, sitting right where they had come to belong on the top shelf of the cupboard beside the cream of tartar.

"It's not the sasanquas," she said, and she tried to explain it to Roger. Her mother, so long gone, and yet . . . And he did seem to understand; he had read somewhere that in other parts of the world people carry their ancestors' bones around with them for generations.

"And I guess the ashes are bones really," said Hilma. She had looked into the tin once, years ago, and had seen that they weren't ashes at all, but little white chips of something you might scatter in a chicken yard to boost the calcium levels of laying hens.

"Comforting! That's ghoulish!" said Meade.

"Not as ghoulish as you could be if you put your mind to it," said Ethel. "Not as ghoulish as making an infusion of the ashes and then drinking off the liquid in the hopes of taking on some of the powers of the deceased. You might try that if you want to be ghoulish."

"Roger said he read that in some parts of the world people keep their ancestors' bones for generations," said Hilma. "They carry them around in richly embroidered cloth bags." Actually, Roger had not mentioned the richly embroidered bags, but Hilma thought embroidery might carry some weight with Meade, who did very fine crewelwork.

"Oh, Roger," said Meade. "Roger would say anything to make you feel better about not doing what you should have done years ago."

They were sitting in Ethel's living room, which had become more like a workshop since the boatwright had come down from New Hampshire. The furniture had all been shoved against the wall to make room for a table saw and a band saw, the bottom half of a dory hung over their heads, and their feet were buried in pine and poplar shavings.

"My," said Hilma, trying to steer the conversation away from the subject of her mother's ashes, "boatbuilding is such a fragrant craft, isn't it, Meade?"

But Meade was thinking. "These bags," she said. "Did Roger say what would be depicted in the embroidery?"

"Oh," said Hilma, thinking fast— "birds." And she began making up ancient traditional designs off the top of her head. "Birds, and they are always depicted with one foot lifted off the ground, symbolizing departure from this life. There's stylized vegetation in the background, palm trees, and those big floppy-leafed things, because these are tropical peoples."

Ethel had put down her sandpaper and was smiling at Hilma with admiration. " 'Peoples,' that's good, Hilma."

"Satin stitch for the plants in cotton, and then the birds in the foreground would be heavy silk or wool to stand out," said Meade. "The bag would have to be a sturdy linen or canvas to last the generations, with those rough bones rattling around in them." Ethel handed her a scrap of sailcloth and she snatched at it lengthwise and on the diagonal. "And French-felled seams, of course. You don't want the ashes sifting out and leaving little trails through the house."

"And the birds," said Ethel, "certain birds would not be appropriate—buzzards, for example."

"She loved the first birds of the fall," said Hilma. "That first flock of robins, on a foggy morning, gobbling up the dogwood berries. How about that, Meade, the dogwood berries would be fun, little red French knots, and the satin-stitched breasts of the robins in a different red."

"I can't embroider a foggy morning," said Meade.

* * *

"Oh, fog is very difficult," Della said earn-estly, "in painting too, although Robert Bateman is famous for it."

"I don't need to see 'bird art,'" Meade had insisted sharply, but Hilma had talked her into this visit with Della, and now here they were, surrounded by crates and boxes and half-finished paintings and drawings, with books and art-gallery brochures spread around the room, talk-ing about birds and depictions of fog in art. Della had served them soggy saltine crackers out of the box. There was no fur-niture, and the only china Hilma could see was a row of mugs on the windowsill that Roger had collected from various phy-topathological meetings. But Meade had not made one comment about the lack of civilized domesticity. And on the way home she only talked about Menoboni and Robert Bateman's fog, and never mentioned Della's odd little habit of pac-ing around and around two of the wooden crates in the middle of the room in a sort of figure eight, her hands clamped under her arms. Now Meade had an abstracted look in her eyes that Hilma remembered from twenty years ago, when she had taken on the job of cross-stitching the

Christian symbol of a fish on twenty-eight kneeling cushions for the altar rail of the Episcopal church, and at the end of ten months they saw that instead of the simple oval and triangle Christian symbol, she had sewn twenty-eight different species of indigenous fish, all recognizable by little stitched details of form and color: warmouth perch, crappie, bluegill, large-mouthed bass.

"She's sewing," Hilma almost whispered to Roger. "Some kind of birds on a canvas bag for the ashes. Every now and then she rushes out to the grocery store and buys a loaf of bread and then darts back in and shuts the door. I'm worried about her eyes. At her age it's not like it was years ago when she did the fishes for the church."

"Art is cruel," said Roger. "I remember when Della was finishing the chickens she didn't eat for a week."

"What have I done?" said Hilma. "Maybe we should have just thrown them into the water in the first place. The fiddler crabs would be chipping away at them right now and growing stronger shells for the winter."

* * *

"It's finished," said Meade, and with a studied nonchalance she pulled the canvas bag out of a paper grocery sack and spread it on the back of the sofa. There was the tiny sound of breaths being held, then silence, and once again Hilma felt the hot tears on her face.

There was her mother's sasanqua tree in full bloom, the ruffled pink blossoms in satin stitch, the yellow stamens in outline stitch. The arching limbs of the tree were filled with fall birds: robins, chipping sparrows, goldfinches, a palm warbler, a white-throated sparrow, and several redbirds. It was late November and the ground under the tree was littered with pink cross-stitched sasanqua petals. The scene was framed by a window, and Hilma recognized the six-over-nine panes of the odd jib windows in her mother's house, now long gone to make way for the parking lot of the Gateway Shopping Center.

Hilma crept away to the kitchen, and soon Ethel came in and stood beside her, and in the living room Roger watched as Della and Meade worked it over.

"Getting the sheen on that damned glass was the hardest part," said Meade. "I tried several things first and had to pick them all out. Featherstitching looked like scum, and a blanket stitch looked like cracks. And I wanted the leaves of the sasanqua to be identifiable, but if I put in too much detail they stood out too much, so I settled for this little serration, which worked out very well."

Della was sitting in front of the sofa on the edge of a straight chair, her elbows on her knees, examining the birds. "The best part," she said, "from the point of view of wildlife art, is the feet."

"Oh, the feet were the very devil," said Meade. "I studied Peterson for hours on those feet."

"Would you believe," said Della, "that many painters, finding them difficult, contrive ways to avoid painting birds' feet? They have them wading in water, or in less realistic work 'implying' feet."

Meade sat down and said fiercely, "You don't mean that!"

In the kitchen Hilma cleared her throat and blew her nose, and Ethel got down cups and saucers while Roger filled the kettle.

"They're both nuts," said Ethel, and Roger smiled at her and said, "Yes, they are."

"We must serve the living, but the dead serve us," Hilma pronounced happily, pouring out tea.

That night before she went to bed, she slid the tin box into the canvas bag and tied up the drawstring top and set it in the cupboard beside the cream of tartar, with the birds facing out so that she would see them every time she made biscuits.

12. IMPASSIONED TYPOGRAPHER

She was carrying two large slices of pale pink watermelon at arm's length. He was following her holding a covered bucket in both hands. It was an unseasonably warm winter day, and she was wearing a sleeveless gray T-shirt and black tights. He was wearing some kind of green cotton robe with ribbed cuffs, and shoes with no socks. The khaki-colored cap crammed onto his head and the big rimless eyeglasses gave his face a studious and concentrated look. They headed out across the garden toward the chicken house.

"Look at the legs on him," said Louise. "What is that he's wearing?"

"Who would buy such a terrible watermelon?" said Eula.

"They didn't know until they cut it," said Ethel.

"What did they expect, a watermelon in the dead of winter?" said Eula. "They're feeding your chickens garbage, Louise." Eula's sink was full of soapy water and dishes, but she wasn't washing anything. She craned her neck to see out the top of the window over the sink.

"Leave the poor people alone," said Ethel. "They came out to the country for privacy, and here we are, scrutinizing them like poultry inspectors."

"Looks like broccoli, some onion peelings, lemons," said Eula.

"My chickens don't eat lemons," said Louise. "Oranges or grapefruits either."

"Oops, he didn't close the gate—yellow hen's out! Headed for your turnip greens, Louise. Watch out, here they all come!" With a grateful surge the little flock of chickens flowed out the gate, then separated, running up and down the garden beds, scratching, pecking, and making the little chortling sounds of delighted chickens.

"Oh, Louise, they're scratching all the mulch off your beds," said Eula, flapping her hands helplessly in the air. The man and woman went to work chasing the chickens, clapping their hands, whooping and laughing. He beetled about with little mincing steps, concentrating on one chicken at a time, lunging forward, doubling back. The ties of his green robe flapped in the breeze. She was more graceful and made chasing chickens look almost like a dance, tracing wide loops with her arms, leaping and swooping.

"Louise, they're stepping in your raised beds," said Eula.

"How much did they pay to spend a month in that house?" said Ethel. "They could run a bulldozer over that garden and you'd still come out ahead."

An arrangement had been made with a Realtor to rent out Louise's house during the winter and spring months. "Enjoy the serenity of country living," the Realtor's ad had said. "Wake to the joyful sound of a cock crowing in the barnyard, gather your own organic vegetables from the garden out back, enjoy romantic evenings by the fire in this antique country home. Convenient shopping in nearby Tallahassee." Even after the Realtor's commission had been deducted, Louise got nearly three hundred dollars a week.

"If that watermelon had been ripe, those chickens would have never left that yard," said Eula.

Finally the man and woman eased the last hen back into the chicken yard and latched the gate. The chickens resumed their methodical and sedate pecking and scratching, and the man and woman leaned on the fence, side by side, watching.

"Now, I understand that," said Eula. "There's something peaceful about watching a flock of chickens pick through garbage." The woman slid an arm around the man's waist and snuggled up against him. The hem of his robe rucked up and exposed the white backs of his knees.

"Look at that," said Louise. "He's cute."

Then the woman nudged the man provocatively with her hip, laughed a throaty laugh, and they sauntered back down the garden path arm in arm, forgetting the garbage bucket. In the chicken yard, a rooster grabbed a hen by the top of the head and mounted her. There was some squawking and flapping, but it didn't last long; the rooster jumped off and instantly resumed his arrogant posture, and the hen stood up, wobbled, growled, bristled her feathers up with a shudder, and went back to her delicate picking at the watermelon rind.

"I'm just as glad he didn't see that," said Eula. "Roosters is too rough."

"Aunt Eula won't leave them alone," Ethel said to Lucy. "At first she just watched them out the kitchen window. Now she's started feeding them. Gingerbread and a beef pie yesterday. Today she's baking bread."

"How do they seem to like it?" asked Lucy. "I mean that drafty old house, for city people, I don't know."

"Listen," said Ethel, "watching a chicken eat a green watermelon makes that woman horny. She never puts her clothes on."

"What's that he's got?" said Eula. "Looks like a piece of a big red 9."

"That's a 'g'," said Louise. "It fell off the

Sunoco sign, 'Regular—$1.09.' That's the 'g' out of Regular."

"Look a there," said Eula. "Now he's got a 8."

"That's a piece of a B," said Louise. "The fat part of a B."

The man was standing out in the yard. He had a screwdriver in one hand and a crowbar in the other. On the ground were piles of sheet-metal scraps, broken pieces of furniture, a tangle of bent wire panels, bits of boards with peeling paint, and a collection of letters and words—parts of wooden and metal signs, single letters and numbers from track signs, and strips of yellow and orange plastic tape with a variety of warning messages: DO NOT ENTER   DO NOT CROSS   DANGER BURIED PIPELINE   STOP DIGGING FIBER OPTIC CABLE BURIED BELOW DO NOT PANIC   LOOK OUT PAINT   AUTHORIZED PERSONNEL ONLY. He kept picking up different things from each pile and turning them around in his hands. Every now and then he would lay a wooden spindle or a section of wire bedspring gently on the ground and walk around it. Sometimes he shifted one piece and laid another piece under it.

Sometimes he stood with his hands on his hips and stared at his piles of stuff.

"Something don't look right to him," said Louise. "He needs something he ain't got."

"What's he doing with all that stuff?" said Eula. "A piece of a screen door, a mashed-up bunch of wire, a pile of run-over sheet metal. They come all the way down here from Kansas City Missouri to pick up junk off the road."

"He's making something out of it," said Louise.

It was early evening, and the woman was in the kitchen mixing up salad greens when Louise knocked on the door.

"It's for him," Louise said. She held her mouth tight and ducked her head down to one side. She was holding an old rusty sheet-metal sign, an advertisement for a defunct brand of dog food. The paint was faded and rust had eroded some of the letters, but you could still see a puppy with big round eyes and a round tongue and the words "Full-O-Pep" arching over his head. "Thought he might could use it for the letters," said Louise.

There was a moment of awkward-
ness—tentative greetings mingled with
bewildered gratitude: "Hi, well, thank you
very much, I'm sure he'll . . . Just put it
over there, he's not . . ." Then the man
came into the kitchen. He took the sign
out of Louise's hands, held it up to the
light, and whistled. He sat down and held
it in his lap. He took a rag from the kitchen
sink and wiped the dust off the arching
letters. Then he looked hard at Louise.

"I'm speechless," he said. "Thank you
very very much."

"It's nothing," said Louise. "I just noticed how you went for that 'g' out of
Regular, thought you could use these. It
come off my brother-in-law's old store,
that's Melvin, Eula's husband, was killed
by his own Allis-Chalmers tractor."

"Oh, I'm so—" said the woman.

"They are absolutely voluptuous," said
the man. "Thank you."

"Well, I'll be going now," said Louise,
and without another word she did go.

"Where did she come from?" asked
the man. He began pacing around the
kitchen, holding the sign up as if it were
a banner in a parade. "Man!" he said,
"Man oh man!"

"She's insane," said the woman.

"Full-O-Pep," he said. "Full-O-Pep." He pushed his salad out of the way. "Look at that toothsome F, that succulent O, that lusty P! Whoa! Look out paint!"

The woman crossed her arms on the table and stared at him. "Bruce," she said.

"You know," he said, turning the sign in his hands and covering sections with a napkin. "If I just . . ."

"Bruce!" she said, but he was rummaging in his tool kit.

"Damn, it's dark," he said, popping the handle of a screwdriver into the palm of his hand. "If you would hold the flashlight—" but she slapped both hands on the tabletop.

"Bruce, you promised me!" she said.

"He's a typographer," the woman said to Eula. "When I first met him he was working for several small publications"—she fixed Eula with a significant look—"and I DO mean small." Between them on the kitchen table a chicken casserole was growing dangerously warm. "The newsletter of the American Gourd Growers Association, *Dairy Goat Journal, Composters'*

Weekly—which meant no money. But he was very passionate about his work, very involved, which is what attracted me to him in the first place." She flung her head back gracefully and ran her fingers through her hair. "So I got him this great job at Hallmark; sure, I pulled some strings—I have connections in Kansas City—but he truly deserved it. They put him to work on a project for a new line of cards called Feelings—really nice, a soft look, flowers, pastels. I don't know what it was—the expectations, the pressure, the responsibility; it's been very intense for him, and when the project was finished I felt we needed this special time away, just for us, a healing time." Eula sat with her hands in her lap thinking of ptomaine poisoning and wondering if it would be impolite to interrupt just long enough to slip the casserole into the icebox.

"... sunsets, long talks around the fireside at night, candlelight . . . But since we've been here I've hardly seen him. He spends all his time making these giant collages out of pieces of junk—signs and pictures and parts of words that don't mean anything." From the backyard they could hear the rasp of a saw as the typographer hacked a yellow capital Y off a fragment of a billboard advertising yogurt. "Sometimes I think he cares more about letters and numbers than he cares about me," the woman said in a frail, wistful voice.

"Oh, honey," said Eula, "you just give him time. He'll come around. Now this casserole—"

"But I want a love that goes beyond the limits of time," she said. In the backyard the typographer laid the Y against a striped board and stood back.

"Just be glad it's letters and numbers and not cockfighting, which is what my Melvin, God bless him . . ." said Eula.

"I'll tell you something," the woman said. "He dreams about typographical styles. He has nightmares about 14-point Eurostile."

"Tiresome woman," said Ethel.

"She needs something to do," said Lucy. "Why don't you suggest gardening, Eula? You could get her started with a gift of seeds."

"She just needs him to pay some attention to her," said Eula. "There he is with that pile of junk, no wonder she feels left out."

"But it's artwork," said Lucy. "As an artist he should get some kind of dispensation."

"Some art!" said Eula. "Bunch of junk screwed together."

"He better watch out or Mama will have the spacemen after him," said Ethel.

"I told Louise not to mention outer space," said Eula. "If she gets on to outer space, they'll be done took back their five thousand dollars and gone."

"I got a S for you today," said Louise, holding out a big black sans serif S. "And some O's. Look a here, this is how they like it." On the ground she laid out a row of black O's printed on clear plastic. She straightened the row, made a tiny adjustment, checked the angle of the sun, and stood back.

"Who?" he asked, settling the big S into one corner of his assemblage.

"I'm not supposed to talk about it," said Louise. "But this is what brings them down; O's and A's and some others, set out east to west."

"Hey," he said, "whatever. I like it." And carefully he laid the row of O's above a black and white picture of Marilyn Monroe with her lips pursed. Then he put an arm around Louise's shoulder and they stood together, just looking. "Whoa!" he said, and he grinned so wide that his cheeks shoved his glasses up the bridge of his nose. "Smokin'!"

"Mistral!" the typographer blurted out, kicking off the covers. "Brush script! No! No!" He moaned and thrashed his head from side to side. Out at the chicken house, one of Louise's insomniac roosters, awakened by the moonlight and the odd cries from the house, rose up, flapped his wings once, and crowed.

Quietly the woman untangled a blanket from the tumbled covers, crept into the living room, and sat in the dark, hugging her knees.

The typographer was out in the backyard, aimlessly walking up and down the chicken yard, picking at the dried brown twigs of vine that clung to the fence. From the ground Marilyn Monroe looked up through Louise's O's, and from the house ostentatious sounds of leaving could be heard—suitcases being flung and dragged across the floor, impetuous footsteps, doors slamming.

"Hey," said Louise. "Today's the day. I got you some A's."

He looked at the A's, but he didn't snatch them up and try them out in different positions, slipping them around from place to place and muttering.

"She's leaving me," he said.

Louise looked around furtively. From the front yard they could hear a car door slam. "Let me tell you something," said Louise.

The woman appeared in the door, her pocketbook on her arm. "Take me to the airport?" she called in a flat, tight voice.

"I'll give her one thing—she sure knows how to leave him," said Ethel. "A few hours of framming and banging and slinging things around, and then vroom! she's gone." It had taken Ethel over a year to leave Roger, counting the months it took to root cuttings from his grandmother's night-blooming cereus.

"I imagine they'll have to do it all over again when they get to their real home," said Lucy. "This leaving was just for show."

"And all because of him screwing numbers and letters and pieces of junk together," said Eula, remembering Melvin's pickup truck coasting silently away from the house under cover of darkness, dozens of fine little wire pens stacked in the back, and then the next morning the dreadful silence and the blood-spattered clothes.

"I imagine it's not just that," said Lucy. "I imagine he was not with her in spirit. It was not a marriage of true minds."

"She's a hard woman," said Eula. "High-strung."

The typographer was leaning up against the kitchen counter drinking whisky, and Louise was making an arrangement on the kitchen table—bits of string, twists of tinfoil, and the letters from a Scrabble game.

"They call it 'Mistral,' " he said. "Syrupy, sappy, insouciantly casual, the George Hamilton of script typefaces—buttoned-down, fetching smile, tan, and oh-so-nice."

"This is my string," said Louise. "The

numbers and letters get their attention and the string brings them on down."

"They take Bodoni," said the typographer, "one of the great typefaces of all time"—he brandished the bottle at Louise, who watched him keenly, her eyes squinted—"and what do they do? They make 'outline' Bodoni. It's like seeing ghosts. They take Gill Sans, a vital, workhorse face—and what do they do? They shorten the uppers, they enlarge the counters, they round off the angles, they make it soft and slack. They castrate it!"

"They come in just as quiet," said Louise. "They just slip in. You don't even know it."

"Insidious is what it is," said the typographer. "We are losing the great typefaces of three centuries, and no one even notices it!"

"You lay your letters down right," said Louise. "Then they come in like water. They come in like air, they seep down from the light. No hole is too small for them little men. When the air is sticky like this? And bristly feeling? You feel that? Come on outside." Louise grabbed the typographer by the arm. "Come on. You'll see it."

It was the end of the unseasonable warm spell. A little breeze was just beginning to stir. It would rain before morning. The warm, damp air felt thick and claustrophobic, trapped as it was between the cold that had been and the cold that was to come.

"You see that light?" said Louise. "You see that?" In the south, over the cotton field across the road, the sky glowed rose and gold where the lights of Tallahassee lit up the undersides of the low clouds.

13. THE AMERICAN LIVESTOCK BREEDS CONSERVANCY

"One thing we can be sure of," Meade said, "that man does not have a single viable sperm in his entire body." The man was the evening's entertainment at the annual conference of the American Livestock Breeds Conservancy. He had a cowboy hat clamped on his head, high-heeled snakeskin cowboy boots, and very tight jeans, the blue paling with stress across his thighs. He was singing "The Tennessee Stud."

Viable sperm had been a recurrent topic at many of the day's meetings, in which the preservation and promotion of endangered breeds of livestock had been discussed. A representative from one of the genetic storage banks for the ALBC had presented a program on fertility evaluation; and Dr. Albert Turner, a renowned professor of animal science, had given a moving talk on the evolution of poultry breeds, pointing out that while the fancy exhibition fowl and the industrial-line egg and meat producers are in no danger, many of the fine old utility breeds from "the Golden Age of Animal Breeding" are almost extinct.

Roger, Della, Hilma, and Meade had driven across the state to attend the conference because Della's painting of Dominique chickens had been bought to hang in the ALBC offices in Pittsboro, North Carolina. Meade had grumbled at first—her interest was in heirloom plants, not livestock breeds. But since she had arrived she had thrown herself into the spirit of the American Livestock Breeds Conservancy, and kept comparing everything to "life."

"Isn't that just like life?" said Meade. "The flashy 'exhibition fowl' thrive and prosper while the venerable old utility breeds are neglected and forgotten."

The country singer had lurched off the

stage in his high-heeled cowboy boots and his tight pants, and Meade, Della, Roger, and Hilma were eating ham sandwiches in the conference-center lounge and discussing Dr. Turner's interesting speech. The tables were shoulder-high, and they had had to scramble up to sit on tall stools, rather like chickens struggling for purchase on a roost, thought Hilma, who couldn't quite figure out where to put her feet. At the next table, she noticed, the president of the Wyandotte Club of America and the manager of a small flock of New Hampshire Reds were perched quite gracefully on their stools, smoking cigarettes and drinking whisky and reading excerpts aloud to each other from a 1922 issue of *Reliable Poultry Journal.*

"But I like the exhibition chickens," Della admitted guiltily. "The spectacular patterns, the flowing tail feathers, the glowing colors."

"You are young, my dear," said Meade. "Someday you will come to appreciate the old and basic things in life."

"Like Meade's old clematis," said Hilma, "a sweet little thing, although I agree with you, Della. The modern ones you see in the plant catalogs are so spectacular, all striped and frilled in those velvety colors."

" 'New and improved,' it always says," said Roger. " 'Hybrid Pride, blooms as big as saucers.' "

"Meade calls them vulgar flowers," said Hilma, almost scornfully, and suddenly Meade felt all alone, as if she had been abandoned in the exalted position Dr. Turner had set up in his speech. Even the serious poultry breeders at the next table had forsaken their noble posts as pre-servers of a genetic heritage, she noticed, and begun to kiss each other, their elbows rumpling the cover of *Reliable Poultry Journal.* Meade felt in her pocket for the envelope of the little "Appomattox clema-tis" seeds she had decided to present as a gift to Dr. Turner. The clematis had been grown in her family's gardens since 1865, when her grandfather had gathered the seed along the road on his long walk home. It was a climber, with little nodding flowers in a delicate shade of pale blue, with a slight, powdery fragrance.

Hilma opened the door of the bedroom just a crack and peered fearfully down the hall. Many of the ALBC members had been housed in this overcrowded bed-and-breakfast inn near the conference center. Some of the larger bedrooms in the old house had been divided in half, and more small rooms had been created by closing in the ends of hallways and porches. Every flat surface was taken up with porcelain figurines of overdressed shepherdesses and their dogs or little homey items edged in eyelet lace, so the guests' coats and bags and cases had to be stacked on the floor or in the seats of chairs, giving a cluttered, claustrophobic feeling to the space.

Hilma crept down the hall, clutching her terry cloth robe to her neck, dreading a bathroom en-counter. At any hour of the night she felt she might turn a corner and run into one of these poultry enthu-siasts, needing to wash up. Sure enough, just as she reached the bath-room, the door opened. But it was only Della, holding a bottle of shampoo in one hand and a tiny lamp in the shape of a leaping fish in the other. "It was on the back of the toilet," said Della, "but it didn't seem quite safe to me—such a damp place for an electrical appliance."

Hilma had an uncomfortable bath, not

quite allowing herself to settle down into the tub, listening for footsteps, voices, and the rattle of the doorknob. When she got back to the room Meade was sitting up in bed, elegantly dressed in a polished-cotton bed jacket, reading *A Conservation Breeding Handbook.*

" 'The loss of these breeds would impoverish agriculture and diminish the human spirit,' " Meade recited. "I do so often feel that my spirit is diminished, Hilma, don't you?" she said.

But Hilma was just feeling damp and frazzled and crowded by knickknacks. "Thank goodness Della got rid of that fish," she said.

It was 4:15 according to the glowing yellow numbers on the little digital clock beside the bed, but Hilma couldn't sleep. She couldn't stop thinking about Meade and her clematis seeds, rare pigs, and the bathroom down the hall. She had overheard the touching presentation of the Appomattox clematis in the hallway, Meade explaining earnestly about the long walk home, and the bowers of clematis over the 130 years in her family's gardens in Virginia,

North Carolina, and now Georgia. Hilma had peeked into the hallway just in time to see Dr. Turner smile and nod and stuff the envelope into his coat pocket while backing up with furtive little steps toward the sanctuary of his own room.

4:29. ". . . successfully imported from England, and now safely in quarantine in New York!" the proud caption had read. But the pigs had looked so pitiful, Hilma thought, nestled together in their straw bed. It would be a concrete room, she supposed, washed down daily with disinfectants. She imagined them lying there, snorting in their sleep, the snout of one pig thrust up against the bristly flank of its neighbor. Did they dream of the home they had left behind in England, she wondered, the green meadows, the hedgerows, the ha-has? Could they have a way of knowing as they slept in that dark and sunless room that they were rare and precious pigs, and that they would soon see another blue sky and root in the damp earth of another continent?

4:36—now would be a good time, she thought, creeping out of bed and picking her way past the piles of shoes and coats to the door. Surely, at this hour no one else would be—

"Oh!" Della yelped with something like relief. "Thank goodness you're awake!" She was leaning against the wall by the bathroom door in her flannel nightgown, fiddling with the doorknob and looking so worried that Hilma forgot about the bathroom and they sat down together among a pile of ruffled cushions on a white satin sofa in the hall. Once again Hilma found herself struggling for a comfortable position. She sat up straight, pressing her toes against the floor to keep from sliding off the domed, slippery seat, and tried to concentrate. But Della wasn't making much sense. It was dark, and she spoke so softly that Hilma could only hear snatches of what she was saying: ". . . warm lumps, covered up in beds," she whispered, ". . . inaccessible thoughts darting around in the dark like bats," and after a while Hilma began to understand that she was describing an unnatural fear she had of sleeping people, something like a dread of snakes or spiders. "Sleepers," Della said with a shudder. "That's why I was so glad to see you."

But there didn't seem to be much comfort Hilma could give her. People did have to sleep, after all. "They will soon wake up, my dear, and be themselves again," said Hilma feebly, "like the Gloucestershire Old Spots pigs coming out of quarantine at last." Then they just sat together on the white sofa until light began to come through the lace curtains, doors opened up and down the hall, and the steady patter to the bathroom began.

Meade lay in her bed and watched the ceiling grow brighter with the dawn, re- membering Dr. Turner's ringing words at the conclusion of his talk: "The challenge of today is to maintain this variability for the entire poultry species, and so protect this genetic heritage for the future." And within the hour the managers of two of the most threatened populations were kissing each other at the supper table, the challenge of today the furthest thing from their minds. Just like life, she thought, snuggling deeper under the cov- ers, people so quickly taken in by the easy pleasures, the flash and strut. *So,* she thought, drifting back to sleep, is such a versatile word, short and simple, and yet powerful when used as Dr. Turner had used it: ". . . and so protect . . ." Dr. Turner had a deep voice, suitable for speaking on the topic of preserving venerable forms of life; and such a fine head of white hair, a strong, expressive nose, almost like a picture of God or Moses. ". . . and so protect . . ." she murmured, thinking of the Appomattox clematis that would bloom next year in his garden.

Conversation was difficult at breakfast. The innkeeper was under the impression that the rare breeds in question were exotic animals and she kept talking on and on about a pink dolphin she had heard about in the Yangtze River. The manager of the New Hampshire flock had not come down to breakfast, and the president of the Wyandotte Club needed a cigarette so badly that his upper lip kept sticking to his teeth, but the words "Thank You for Not Smoking" were printed on a blue plywood goose screwed to the wall over every door. Della wanted a glass of water, but only pale coffee was offered, and Dr. Turner, in his rightful place at the head of the table, kept striking his knees against the gatelegs hidden under the damask tablecloth.

"Very, very rare," the innkeeper said enthusiastically, pouring lukewarm coffee out of a silver coffeepot. "Only about fifty of them left in the world, dolphins are so cute anyway, and a PINK one, I just can't imagine—you all do such important work, saving these poor animals from extinction."

But the nerves of the president of the Wyandotte Club were too frazzled for more talk of pink dolphins, and he suddenly blurted out in an angry voice, "I am a poultryman!"

"Oh!" the innkeeper yelped, and she hastily set down a platter of quivering poached eggs and disappeared into the kitchen.

There was a tense moment as everyone stared at the eggs, adjusting to the silence. But Hilma took up the platter bravely and passed it graciously to Dr. Turner, saying, "I certainly hope these are not the eggs of a rare and endangered flock."

"No," said Dr. Turner, just as everyone began to relax. "I would say that this egg was laid by a White Leghorn hen, crammed into a space no bigger than your two hands. Her beak may have been cut off when she was one day old to keep her from pecking her cage mates, or she might have been fitted at eighteen weeks of age with a pair of red contact lenses." Then, as everyone sat with their hands in their laps, Dr. Turner explained that hens in such numbers are not able to establish their social order, and have a tendency in their frustration to peck one another to death. The red contact lenses, by filtering out the color of blood, reduce this social stress, eliminating cannibalism, increasing egg production, and so resulting ultimately in a significant improvement in the feed-conversion ratio.

"And it is to this impoverished state that the noble science of avian husbandry has sunk," Dr. Turner concluded with a smack.

After that there was a little nibbling at pieces of dry toast, but no one felt like talking. At last Roger made a move, pushing his chair back and saying, "Well," and then everyone got up with relief and hurried back to their rooms to pack.

Hilma stuffed her things into her suitcase and then sat in a chair by the window looking out at the gray day while Meade spread clothes out on the bed and folded them up with tissue paper.

There had been something uncomfortable and troubling about the ALBC conference, Hilma decided—those spotted
pigs she couldn't get off her mind,
Meade's odd remark about feeling diminished in her spirit, and then Della's
strange night terrors. "Sleepers," she had
whispered with such horror.

Outside in the parking lot, people shiv-
ered in the light, cold mist, holding newspapers over their heads and loading
bags into the trunks of cars.

"Oh, look," said Hilma, "there's Dr.
Turner," and Meade stopped her packing.
He certainly was a handsome man for his
age, Hilma thought, such a noble mien.
She watched as he fumbled in his coat
pockets. But instead of keys, he pulled out
Meade's little white packet of clematis
seeds. He stood there looking at it, as if
he were trying to remember where it had
come from. Meade had begun picking her
way carefully through the piles of bags
and shoes to the window, but Hilma had
the presence of mind to say quickly, "Oh,
never mind, it's just some other—" and
Meade turned back to her packing just as
Dr. Turner flipped the envelope open and
shook the little seeds out in the rain.

14. IN THE BLEAK MIDWINTER

"A great fan," said Jim Wade, "sixteen-inch, side-winder oscillator." He slid the lever to High, and the fan wearily lumbered into action. It took a while, but by the time it got going, Christmas cards were flying across the room, and Ethel could feel tears blowing out of the corners of her eyes. "Now what do you think," Jim Wade said, "is that the world's greatest fan, or what?"

It was a 1919 General Electric, three speeds, with copper blades that showed up as a golden glow at the root of the gale. One of the blades had a jagged chipped edge that threw the fan a little off-balance and set up a vibration that caused the whole store to rattle and shake. A pair of Mr. and Mrs. Santa salt and pepper shakers marched with wobbly steps to the edge of their shelf. Ethel caught Mrs. Santa (salt) just as she began to tip.

"Let her go," said Jim Wade. "Tacky consignment junk. Let her hit that concrete floor and smash into a thousand pieces. People bring this stuff in here, expect me to sell it. And you know the saddest thing, Ethel? I do sell it." He slid the switch to Medium, then Low, and stood by the fan with his eyes closed.

"I can see this fan in your house, Ethel, on Low, a summer night. I see a tomato sandwich, a jar of capers; the doors are open to the evening breeze, nothing but the sound of crickets."

But it was December, Ethel was looking for a woodstove, not an electric fan, and in the background chipmunks were singing "Silent Night."

"Jim Wade," said Ethel, sliding the switch back to Off. "It was fifteen degrees last night. No one wants to hear about the evening breeze."

"It's a habit of mine," said Jim Wade wistfully, "daydreaming in other seasons.

Do you daydream in other seasons, Ethel?" But in a far corner of the store Ethel had found a beautiful woodstove, with a nickel-plated fender and a gleaming finial.

"Oh no!" Jim Wade said, swooping in on her, "Oh no!" He stood in front of the stove and held Ethel off with one hand. "A great old stove from the 1890s, you're thinking to yourself? Maybe Birmingham Iron Works, you're thinking to yourself? You *think*"—he paused dramatically—"made in Taiwan, early eighties—NINETEEN-eighties. See this? Phillips-head screws. Junk! An imitation of nothing that ever existed, designed by tricksters to bring back memories that nobody ever had. Three hundred and fifty dollars, a ridiculous price for a fake stove. And you know what, Ethel? Some woman will come in here wearing a green dirndl skirt and a shirt with red piping on the collar and buy the thing! She'll put an arrangement of artificial flowers on the lid. Flowers on top of a woodstove, Ethel, just think about it! Country charm!"

"Oh, Jim Wade," said Ethel. " 'Tis the season to be jolly."

"Ethel," said Jim Wade, "one thing and one thing only would make me jolly."

"Don't start, Jim Wade," said Ethel. "Help me find a woodstove. I want to heat my house with boat scraps."

"The stove you want isn't here," said Jim Wade, and he flipped the sign on the Antique Mall to CLOSED and locked the door. "The stove you want is a Columbus Stove and Range model—a Little Bungalow—out at Paramore Surplus."

Jim Wade turned on the heat in his van and they roared through town, past the Christmas tree on the courthouse lawn, past the Salvation Army woman in her short red skirt prancing up and down in the cold on the corner of Jackson and Broad, past the ten-thousand-dollar display of lights at Flowers Industries, and out onto Highway 84.

"Marry me, Ethel!" cried Jim Wade, turning loose of the steering wheel and slapping the dashboard with both hands. "This spring, in St. Louis, the fan-manufacturing capital of the U.S., marry me!"

"You missed it," said Ethel. "You should have turned on 111."

* * *

"Got a nice fan out back," said Mrs. Paramore, glaring up at Jim Wade. "Old Emerson model." Her stringy, blue-veined feet, in silver lamé slippers, were propped up on a little gas space heater, and a pair of Santa Claus earrings swung violently from her weary earlobes. Ethel found the woodstove under a pile of tin bathtubs half full of rusty ice water and frozen mosquito wigglers, and bloodied her knuckles untangling it from a pile of copper and iron weather vanes—roosters and trotting horses and a cow and a pig pointing north, south, east, and west.

"Twenty-five for the stove, fifty-five dollars for the fan, firm," said Mrs. Paramore, clamping her thin lips onto her cigarette and crossing her arms over the skinny blue iron-on Victorian Santa Claus on her sweatshirt. "That's an Emerson."

"But look at this oil cup!" wailed Jim Wade. "Look at this cheap motor! This is not the fine hollow-core Emerson motor of the twenties and thirties! This is a wartime Emerson!"

Ethel left her money on the counter, and in the parking lot she made a ramp out of two two-by-sixes and heaved and shoved the stove into the back of Jim Wade's van.

"Look at this wrinkle finish!" Jim Wade's voice rang out across the grim fields of scrap metal, car parts, and pieces of houses. "Look at this cross guard!"

"It's an Emerson fan. My prices is firm," smacked Mrs. Paramore. The Santa Claus earrings snatched and bobbed emphatically, stretching the holes in her earlobes to vicious little slits. "I don't dicker."

"I swear, Ethel," said Jim Wade, roaring back down Highway 84, "I should be under the care of a psychoanalyst, or at the very least I should be spending six hours a day under a 200-watt bulb reading the short stories of Somerset Maugham."

"Seasonal affect disorder, that's what they call it," said Ethel, nursing her scraped knuckles.

"Instead I'm eking my life away down in that store," said Jim Wade, "selling male-end-only strings of Christmas lights to overweight women dressed in clothes that blink. I'm a danger to myself and others, Ethel. So watch out."

At Ethel's house they struggled with the stove up the stairs to the strains of "Joy to the World" wafting across the park from the loudspeakers downtown. Ethel began snapping sections of stovepipe together while Jim Wade unscrewed the oil cup on her little Emerson Seabreeze.

"Who but you, Ethel, would know to use Royal Purple?" he sighed. "Look at this"—and he spread his arms and made a slow spin. The elegant little sailboat hung in a sling from the ceiling, and one corner of the room was filled with wood scraps in neat stacks, but the Portsmouth boatbuilder had taken his tools back to New Hampshire early in the fall and Ethel had swept up the shavings and sawdust and put the furniture back. "No garlands of greenery, no stockings hung by the chimney with care, no bandsawed plywood reindeer prancing across the wall," said Jim Wade, "just the simple, functional home of a capable woman who knows how to take care of an Emerson desk fan."

"Get your side," said Ethel, snapping in the last section of pipe, and together they lifted the stove up and settled it into place. Ethel jammed the elbow into the ceramic thimble and stood back.

"Wooo!" she said, crumpling up newspapers and stuffing scraps of poplar and pine into the little front door of the stove. "Give me a match, Jim Wade, turn off that fan!"

Behind the little isinglass window of the stove door the flames flickered and danced. It was cold outside, another freezing night. Ethel had brought her plants in, and the warmth from the stove spread the rich loamy smell all through the room. Jim Wade started water boiling for tea while Ethel checked the tightness of the stovepipe joints with gloved hands.

"I will never understand the mystique of boats," said Jim Wade. "All that business about the lonely sea and the sky and a star to steer her by. To me it just seems damp and cold, with an enormous potential for danger. Was that it, Ethel, that heady feeling that is said to come over us right before a violent death? Because I never could figure it out, to me he just seemed like a bandy-legged little man with a funny-looking saw, he never said anything, and he always smelled like glue every time I saw him. What I want to know, Ethel, is, why did it have to be boats in particular, instead of, say, electric desk fans?"

"It doesn't have anything to do with boats or fans, Jim Wade," said Ethel. "Stop trying to figure it out."

The wood scraps were very dry, and the fire had gotten so hot that the stove had begun making rhythmic sucking gulps: whomp whomp whomp.

"Here we are, two lonely people huddled around a pitiful spark," Jim Wade said. " 'Earth as hard as iron, water like a stone.' "

"I am not lonely, Jim Wade," said Ethel, closing the vent down hard and snapping the damper shut. "And this is not a pitiful spark. We may see flashover any second now."

" 'In the bleak midwinter,' " said Jim Wade.

"The bleak midwinter has its benefits," said Ethel. "Just think of the fleas that might have tormented dogs and cats next July, now being killed by this cold snap."

The roaring in the stove settled down to a low rustling murmur. Ethel and Jim

Wade sat drinking their tea and listening to the little clicks and taps and rumbles as the stove adjusted to its heat and the firewood slumped into the ashes.

Then, inspired perhaps by the gleaming blades of the well-oiled Emerson Seabreeze, or the summery smells of green plants, or the flickering glow through the little window in the door of the stove—the last remnants of the Portsmouth boatwright going up in smoke, Jim Wade leaned over and gave Ethel a kiss. But it was an ill-placed kiss that landed on the angle of her jaw, and Jim Wade was left with the impression of a hard, sharp edge against his lips.

His van didn't have time to warm up on the short drive to his house, and he sat at the stoplight, feeling the cold wrap around his legs, and tried to imagine himself heading west on 84, away from all the glitter and sparkle of Christmas, through the narrow winter days, and right out the other side to summertime in some vast midwestern state where the blades of electric fans would spin and the air would be filled with the hum of their hollow-shaft motors—Zephair, Northwind, Seabreeze, Vortalex, Star

Rite. But it was cold and dark—the bleak midwinter—and as he drove past the tiny white lights twinkling so cheerily on the azalea bushes in the park, he found that he couldn't think about anything but the deaths of fleas.

15. BETTY SHEFFIELD SUPREME

"Who is Betty Sheffield?" asked Della. " 'Betty Sheffield' is a variety of camellia with semidouble blossoms, white with red and pink splotches on the petals. It's a nice camellia, but it's most famous for producing many fine mutations, called 'sports,' " said Roger.

"Oh," said Della, looking out the car window for a wood stork. Sometimes when she thought about seeing a certain bird she could develop such a longing for it that her eyes would smart and the spit would change texture at the back of her tongue. All day she had been wanting to see a wood stork against this gray sky, but there she had been since the morning, at a camellia show, shut up in that long room with rows and rows of flowers in glass jars and hundreds of men and women stooping over each one, clutching sweaters around themselves and saying strange-sounding words: 'Alba Plena,' 'Mathotiana Rubra,' 'Betty Sheffield,' and 'Betty Sheffield Supreme.' Deep rose pink, ruby red, glowing crimson, pink stripes, red splotches, pink shading into white and white shading into rose, frilled petals and scalloped petals, and petals with elaborate ragged edges; all that richness, thought Della, when what I need is so very simple, just black and white and gray, that sharp clean shape against the sky. Sometimes in her painting she would get the same feeling, an anxious longing for something to come out right—the primary and secondary feathers sharp, but not overdone with outlining, the drop of water on a lily pad fat and round and shiny, but not detracting from the eye of the nearby moor hen, also round and shiny, and as she came at the paper with the brush, she would have to stop for a second and blink and swallow. It was a desperate, helpless feeling, as if in spite of her skill she had no more control over those feathers or that drop of water than she had over the wood storks in north Florida on a winter day.

She leaned up against the car window and watched the telephone wires swoop and lift and swoop and lift. If I see a wood stork before we get to the store, then I will be able to finish the upper right-hand section, she thought. It was a difficult tangle of pickerelweed, with sunlight shining through the leaves. But the store came and went, with a flashing sign, "Christmas Sausage on Sale 2-Day," and there were only a few doves and a king-fisher on the telephone wire. It was almost dark and Della leaned back in the seat and closed her eyes through Panacea with its crab houses and the laboratories of the Marine Institute, and then, just on the other side of town where the marsh starts up again, Roger stopped the car and said, "Look!" Della gulped and scrambled for her binoculars, peering through the windshield into the last light. There on a stump in the ditch was a bald eagle, so fat and complacent it looked almost stuffed. "Oh," said Della, and she slumped back in the seat, trapped by a longing for birds.

"Why in the world did you take her to a camellia show on such a dreary day?" said Meade. "What could be worse for depression than a room full of little old ladies all fussing over the 'Betty Sheffield Blush' and the 'Betty Sheffield Supreme'?"

"For the flowers," said Roger. "It always worked with Mrs. Maxwell. You should have seen her face brighten up every time I set those roses down on the railing at Shady Rest."

"Mrs. Maxwell was ninety-eight years old, Roger," said Meade. "She was dying. Her needs were simple."

"I miss Mrs. Maxwell," said Roger.

"Of course Della didn't enjoy the flower show," said Hilma. "So claustrophobic with all the people and that gray thick fog outside." She sat still and thought for a minute. "I know what; Meade and I will take her to Maclay Gardens on a high, bright, windy day and walk around among those ancient camellias."

And so they had fought the after-Christmas traffic to walk Della down the wide brick paths of this old camellia garden. Some of the bushes were over a hundred years old and formed a towering canopy overhead, casting a dense, cold shade. The bricks were slippery with damp.

"'Mathotiana Rubra,'" said Hilma, "an old one, but not one of my favorites. They turn purple at the edges as they die."

"The dead ones look just as good as the live ones," said Della. The ground under the bushes was littered with deep rose and purple and finally brown, the blossoms retaining their perfect "imbricated double" form even in decay.

"Heartless flowers," said Meade, "contrived by foolish people for their own amusement. They have no fragrance."

"Ah," said Hilma, "here it is." In the middle of a patch of bright green rye grass a full camellia bush was covered with semidouble white blossoms, each petal neatly bordered with deep pink. "The prized 'Betty Sheffield Supreme,'" said Hilma, and she picked up a spent blossom off the ground and handed it to Della.

"Winner of the Sewell Mutant Award," said Meade.

"A most unusual camellia, and very rare," said Hilma. "Roger has had his name on a list at Hjort's for years, but crooked collectors keep slipping in ahead of him."

Della poked at the quivering yellow stamens with a finger and sniffed it, but all she could detect was a coolness rising up out of the petals.

"See?" said Meade. And suddenly, among all the pink and white, a bright smiling face appeared, and a voice cried out.

"Oh! Here she is, my wonderful painter!" Then there were two of the faces. "This is Della, Maryann, she's painting a beautiful picture for our den, a wildlife scene, it's supposed to be a surprise, Herbert commissioned it for my birthday, but I can already see it in my mind, she does the most wonderful things with light. Her pictures have been exhibited at the same show where the duck-stamp painting is displayed every year, and that painting sells for over a million dollars. Luckily for us, Della doesn't command quite that figure yet, do you, Della? Oh, how appropriate to see you here, surrounded on all sides by beauty; it must make you want to just go right home and paint paint paint paint paint."

And then just as suddenly the talking stopped, and the two women looked expectantly from Della to Hilma and Meade. But Della stood there helplessly, holding the bright dead flower in her hand, and seeing in her mind a full third of the whole painting blank, a startling white gap sketched over with little dim, frightened-looking pencil lines, and in the end Hilma had to step in. There was the lighthearted sentence to smooth over the awkward pause, then the necessary remark about the beauty of the gardens, and then the introductions were begun.

"I am Hilma Martin, a friend of Della's, and this is—" But before she could continue, Meade stepped forward, plucked the flower out of Della's hand by its bunch of stamens, hurled it over her shoulder, and said in a loud voice, "Betty Sheffield is my name."

"Meade . . ." said Hilma, feebly trailing off, and Della stared down at her empty palm. A few parting remarks were thrown out, and they watched the two women saunter down the brick walkway toward the Maclay House.

"Betty Sheffield!" said Hilma, recovering herself. "My goodness, Meade!"

"I couldn't help it," said Meade. "There we stood, ankle-deep in the dead blossoms of 'Betty Sheffield Supreme.' It just slipped out."

"But how would Betty Sheffield feel, having her name tricked about like that?" Hilma persisted. "It's not respectful."

"Betty Sheffield is dead," said Meade. "And besides, she's used to hearing her name tripping off the tongues of camellia fanciers on three continents."

Then Della held up both hands. "Wait," she said. "There is a real Betty Sheffield? It's not just a name? A real woman was named Betty Sheffield?"

"Yes," said Hilma, "a lovely little lady. She lived in Quitman with her sister. The original 'Betty Sheffield' camellia came up in her yard as a seedling."

"She lived in Quitman with her sister?" said Della breathlessly. "Betty Sheffield? And now she's dead?"

"Oh yes," said Hilma. "She registered the camellia in 1948, and she wasn't a young woman then. It wasn't until it started throwing all these sports that it got so much attention. It was Mrs. Green Alday's Betty Sheffield that sported the first 'Betty Sheffield Supreme.'"

A few robins were scratching in the rye grass vista. Della sat down on a cast-iron bench and stared down toward Lake Hall. Her eyes began to water, and she felt the spit thicken at the back of her tongue.

"What was her sister's name? Is her house still there?"

"Somewhere in downtown Quitman," said Hilma, "and her sister had an odd name, but why, and what—"

"Court Street," said Meade. "A Queen Anne house with front- and side-crossed gables and a wrought-iron fence around the yard."

"I don't understand it," Hilma said to Roger. "I don't understand it, Roger. Meade hates camellias, and Della seemed quite indifferent, even at Maclay Gardens with all those specimen plants. Then Meade flew off on some wild tear in the garden about Betty Sheffield and her sister with the odd name, and Della fell right in with her. She really seemed to brighten up, Roger, and next thing I knew, off they went to Quitman, to Court Street. I don't understand it. Come in out of the cold, Roger. Wasn't this your fungicide night in Pelham? You must be tired."

Roger sat down on Hilma's sofa in the middle of the winter clutter—the dog-eared seed catalogs, the tray of tea things, and the Boston ferns brought in from the cold. He took off his shoes and stretched his legs. Hilma was concerned about him; he recognized the signs—the fussings to make him comfortable with afghans and pillows, the little glances, and her face so worried. He knew that the tea would be Earl Grey from a tin, not just tea bags from Publix. He could smell the bergamot.

"Odette was the name of Betty Sheffield's sister," said Roger.

"I told Della that you would know that," said Hilma. "Such an odd name."

But it wasn't a conversation that they could really take hold of, and after a few minutes of silence Roger said, "I'm an ordinary man, Hilma. All day long I study cause and effect. I'm good at it, but it's not helping me."

"Oh, Roger," said Hilma, and she almost stood up, and then sat back down again and put her teacup down and fumbled with her hands in her lap. They sat for a while, not saying anything. Then, "I want to give you something," Roger said, and without even putting on his shoes, he went out to his truck and came back with a little camellia bush in a black plastic pot.

"I finally got my 'Betty Sheffield Supreme' from Hjort's," he said, "but I want you to have it."

It was supposed to be for Della, thought Hilma, but all she could say was, "Oh, Roger," and "Thank you."

It had a few tightly closed buds, not showing color yet, but 'Betty Sheffield' camellias are famous for throwing out odd sports, and they would have to wait until it bloomed to see what a fine mutant this little plant would be.

16. VECTORED BY THRIPS

"That spotted wilt is going to be the death of you, Roger," said Eula, "all these meetings late at night in every little town, typing into that computer hours on end all those articles about thrips, and every summer day stooped over in the peanut field, steeped in sweat. If you don't get snakebit first, you're going to die of exhaustion. 'Vectored by thrips,' now what is a thrip, Roger, I don't even know that."

"Thrips," said Roger. "Even if you're talking about just one, it has an 's' on the end. Thrips are the insects that spread the virus among the peanut plants. Tiny little things, you can hardly see them."

"Well, damn their little souls, Roger," said Eula.

They were on their way home from the Agricenter in Calvary, where Roger was holding a series of Thursday night meetings with peanut farmers on the subject of tomato spotted wilt virus. "Eula needs to get out some," Lucy had told him. "Louise is driving her crazy with all this talk of spacemen, Tom had another fight on the long-distance telephone with Judy about Andy, and she worries about Ethel. Eula needs something to get her mind off it."

So Roger had invited Eula to come with him to his peanut meeting, and there she had sat for over an hour, bolt upright on a folding chair in the front row at the Agricenter with all the Grady county peanut farmers, listening so attentively it almost broke his heart.

Now on the ride home she was perched on the edge of the seat of his truck, hanging on to the dashboard with both hands. "Fasten your seat belt, Eula," Roger told her. "You never know what kind of drivers might be out on these roads this time of night." And then, strapped in, she settled down a little and seemed to relax.

"Now this is nice, Roger," she said. "Riding along in this truck with you, seeing them plowed fields stretching out in the night. Before you know it it'll be summer and you'll be walking down those very rows in the hot sun, looking for sickly plants." Actually, the very rows Roger would be walking down were in the research plots in Attapulgus, the next county over, but Eula had a thought going, and he didn't interrupt her. "Andy will be here, God willing and Judy don't pitch a fit, Ethel will be out of school, I'll have my tomatoes in; it's something to look forward to, ain't it, Roger?"

They rode on in silence for a while, past the bleak-looking fertilizer plant outside Bainbridge, past Jones Meats with its flashing sign in Climax. Roger thought Eula was asleep, but then she said, "Thrips, with an 's.' Now you learn something new every day, don't you, Roger."

She invited Roger in, but he better get home, he said, and probably a good thing, she thought as she crept around in the kitchen making herself a cup of Ovaltine to take to bed, better not to wake up Louise with talking. Night was no different than day to Louise; if she got waked up in the middle of the night, she would go right to bustling around with her crazy schemes and not stop until noon the next day. But sometimes when the house was quiet like this, Eula could almost imagine that she lived here alone, like in the old days, after Melvin died, before Louise lost her mind and Tom moved back home. She sat up for half an hour, sipping her Ovaltine and thinking about Roger standing up there at the Agricenter, all those serious-looking peanut farmers sitting in chairs lined up in rows, listening to him.

It had a noble sound to it, "vectored by thrips," she thought. Roger had always reminded her of a prince, ever since he had come back from that university in North Carolina, bald-headed and with a Ph.D., and married Ethel. "Vectored by thrips," she whispered to herself, "with an 's.'"

"She wasn't even his mother-in-law," said Meade.

"Well," said Hilma, "you can't really think of Louise as anybody's mother. Eula was the one who raised Ethel, after all. I would certainly consider her Roger's mother-in-law."

"Ex-mother-in-law," said Meade.

"She's a good woman," said Hilma, "and now she has all these worries. Tom is no help to her, always flying off the handle, and now they say his wife Judy out in California has caught this sickness where she can't do anything for herself. I wouldn't be surprised if Eula ended up having to take on Andy to raise, just like she took on Ethel."

"Ex-wife," said Meade.

"And on top of it all, there's Louise," said Hilma. "Roger might be able to take her mind off it with these peanut meetings."

Roger was standing beside a chart at the Agricenter explaining the factors of the tomato spotted wilt virus "risk index": peanut variety, planting date, planting density, location of field, volunteer peanut population from previous crops, and at-planting thrips control. "Add the numbers for the factors that apply to your planting and compare that total to the numbers in the scale to find out your projected relative level of risk for TSWV," said Roger. Then everybody had a question to ask and five or six men all said

"Roger" at the same time, and Roger smiled and held up his hands and then answered the questions one at a time. "I wish we could tell you more," he said. "It's slow."

"I felt so proud, Roger," said Eula, as they drove home. "All those men sitting so still and listening to you like they was memorizing every word you said."

"They're worried about their peanut crop," said Roger. "They think the cure for this epidemic might come out of our research, and they're disappointed when all we can tell them is ways to manage the virus."

"A ten," said Eula. "I couldn't help but notice my own county had a 10 on the scale where it said 'location of field.' "

"The southwest counties have been hit hard," said Roger.

Louise was up when Eula came in, sitting at the kitchen table arranging a trail of Cheerios and the letters from a Scrabble game on a sheet of heavy-duty aluminum foil. "Well," she said, "H, U, Y, and M. That should do it."

"I've been to Roger's Thursday night peanut meeting in Calvary," said Eula. "Tomato spotted wilt virus. TSWV they call it. Vectored by thrips, with an 's.' Roger says it has spread quicker than any plant disease he's ever seen, and here we are, sitting in the middle of Grady County, with a ten on the index scale. Lumpkin only had a five."

"S," said Louise, and she just kept lining up letters and Cheerios along a piece of string against a wrinkle in the foil; she would never stop once she started that, so Eula made sure all the doors were locked, put on her nightgown by the heater, and got into her bed. Tomorrow she would send Andy a box of cheese straws and pecans, she thought. His mother Judy had taken hold of the notion that she was being slowly poisoned by every single thing she ate, and for over a month now she had eaten only brown rice and dates. If Tom would just keep from saying cruel things on the long-distance telephone, Judy would let Andy come to them in June when school was out. They would drive over to Jacksonville to meet the airplane. But a child could starve to death between January and June on nothing but brown rice and dates.

Sometimes when Eula closed her

eyes she could see Andy's face—the freckles, the two big front teeth, still looking new and overlapping a little bit just like Melvin's used to do. But this night when she closed her eyes, all she could see were the anxious faces of the farmers at the Agricenter, their chapped, cold hands clasped in their laps, and Roger holding on to the edge of the lectern, looking weary, and in the background a color photograph of a yellowed and withering peanut plant, little black round holes in its leaves edged in white.

"Eula certainly is getting an education in virology," said Lucy. "Ethel says all she can talk about is TSWV. Ethel says she's worse than you were."

"At first she was just excited to be away from home, and she liked the long words," said Roger. "But now she's started following the discussion. Last week she asked a question about resistant varieties."

"Tom talked to Judy last night," said Lucy. "He lost his temper and said something that made her mad, and she told him that Andy's personal growth has been stunted because of the sharp contrast between his two homes. He's using up all his energy making the transition, and doesn't have any left over to develop as a human being, she says. So she wants to send Andy to something called a personal awareness camp. They only eat the purest kinds of food, and the little children have to sit around a campfire at night and look inward."

"Good Lord," said Roger.

"Eula's afraid Andy might not be able to come this summer," said Lucy. "So give her a chance to talk about it on Thursday."

That Thursday night was the last of the peanut meetings in Calvary. Roger called Eula and said, "Don't eat any supper tonight. We'll eat at the Pastime on the way home."

The title of Roger's talk on this last night was "Living with Tomato Spotted Wilt Virus." "It's important to understand that the risk index is not a cure," said Roger. "If you take the recommended actions to lower your risk, it doesn't mean you won't get the virus. It just means that your risk of damage is relatively lower." There was a little talk of a new cultivar,

'Georgia Browne,' which had shown some resistance. But the farmers seemed restless and dissatisfied. In the front row a small Donald Duck orange juice can beside someone's chair got kicked over and tobacco juice trickled across the polished concrete floor of the Agricenter.

"It may not be this summer; it may not be for ten more years," said Roger. "But there's enough virus out there that we have the potential for an explosive outbreak." Then the meeting was over, and the peanut farmers shuffled around, collecting their coats, swiping their hair back under their caps, and messing up the rows of chairs. Most of them shook hands with Roger solemnly and some of them nodded good-bye to Eula.

On the drive to Cairo, Roger tried several times to broach the topic of Andy and the personal growth camp. But Eula wouldn't stop talking about peanuts. "Georgia Browne, now that's a nice name for a peanut," she said. "I wonder why they put that 'e' on the end of it. Too bad about the kernels being so small, Roger."

It was late when they got to the Pastime, and Fern brought them plates piled high with food. "You're helping us clean up," she said. "If I didn't feed it to you, I'd have to throw it out."

Eula poked around in the mashed potatoes and made a stab at her pork chop, but her heart wasn't in it. She said, "A peanut ain't just a peanut anymore, is it, Roger?" and he agreed that with the new advanced breeding lines and cultivars there did seem to be more to it than there used to be.

"No matter what you do to fix it, the trouble just keeps on spreading out in front of you," said Eula.

"Don't hurry, Roger," said Fern. "I'm just going to turn off the open sign, but y'all take your time. We've got plenty to do in the kitchen."

By the time they left, the traffic lights had been turned to just blink red, on and off.

"Why, it's that late," said Eula.

Roger's truck was the only moving vehicle in town, and they rolled slowly down Broad Street, pausing at each blinking light. The pavement was slick and damp. He would sleep for a few hours, Roger thought, and then he would go out and collect some predawn-darkness dew for his water agar plates, before the morning breezes contaminated it with spores and pollen.

Eula sat quietly, her hands in her lap, looking straight ahead down the gleaming black road. But she was not thinking about Andy eating dates and brown rice in California, or about Tom snarling into the long-distance telephone, or about the beetle man coming up on the porch calling "Ma'am, ma'am," and Louise hanging back on the steps all scratched up and mumbling about a string to Mars. Instead she was thinking about a field of peanuts in early summer, and about a tiny fluttery thing, almost invisible, flying into all that greenness on little feathery wings, and about the clusters of destruction that were sure to follow.

17. THE DYING HOUSE

"Drip it until you have a stream the size of a pencil," the plumber told Hilma, and she sat down primly on the edge of the toilet with her hands in her lap and watched dutifully as he adjusted the trickle by tapping the handles impatiently with his rough red knuckles, first the hot, then the cold.

This had been the coldest winter since records had been kept, with arctic front after arctic front rolling down from Canada. Hilma had always dripped the spigots until the drops almost touched, like beads slipping off a string, but this year that was not enough; pipes had burst and she had had to call this impatient young plumber. Now as she lay in bed under two blankets and a quilt listening to the gurgle of water from the bathroom and kitchen, she could almost imagine that she was visiting some tropical grotto, green with ferns and moss. But then she smelled the rubbery winter smell of the hot-water bottle, and felt the icy breeze creeping under the door, and saw on the window shelf the little spindly seedlings she had prematurely started in flats, grasping desperately for the thin light that streamed into the bedroom for a few minutes every morning. She had not sterilized the soil, and in this cold weather the seedlings were susceptible to "damping off." Every morning Hilma would find a few more little plants toppled over, lying on the dirt with the base of their stems pinched and blackened.

"Damping off," said Hilma, and wondered if she too might not keel over one February night and be found the next morning by Meade or Lucy or Roger, stretched out in her nightgown on the floor, surrounded by trickles of water the size of pencils, and flats of seedlings optimistically labeled for planting out on a fine spring morning: Canterbury Bells, Dame's Rocket, Forget-Me-Not.

"Cheer up," Meade told her roughly. "You are allowing dismal thoughts to occupy your mind like bad-smelling old men on a bus. You should have sterilized the soil—this cold weather has activated the soil pathogens. Now you must start over. And this time you will enjoy your success more, knowing that you have done your best."

Hilma sighed. She would have to start over. And as she dumped out all the little pots of soil, she thought how merciless are these tiny cold-weather enemies, and how hard-fought are all the small triumphs of winter.

But the next morning was bright; ice was actually thawing in the birdbath, and the kitchen was filled with the humusy smell of the soil baking in the oven—350 degrees for one hour to kill the soil pathogens. Hilma was feeling almost cheerful when Meade arrived with the sad news.

"I have terrible news," Meade announced, standing in the doorway very straight, her hands clasped in an official-looking position just under her chest,

"Oh," said Hilma weakly, reaching for the back of a chair. She felt breathless; someone has died, she thought, and suddenly she remembered the smell of rosemary and wild azalea that had filled the church at her mother's funeral forty years ago.

"Squeaky is dying," said Meade in a low, throaty voice.

"Oh," said Hilma, sinking into the chair. Squeaky was Roger's beloved childhood horse, who had already lived to the incredible age of thirty-five years. Hilma pictured the dead horse lying on its side, flattened against the ground by its own weight, and in the foreground, like credits at the movies, appeared the faces of dear friends who were not dead or dying: Ethel, Lucy, Roger, Mr. Rice down at the birdseed store, even the nice man with the twinkly smile at the library—all still alive and well. It seemed almost as if Squeaky had been sacrificed that others might live.

"Oh," said Hilma, "poor Squeaky."

"Poor Squeaky!" snapped Meade. "Squeaky should have died fifteen years ago. 'Poor Roger' is what you mean. I'm terribly worried about Roger. What's that smell?"

"Oh," said Hilma, "I'm killing soil pathogens." And it seemed as if they were surrounded on this bright winter day by the deaths of creatures both large and small.

"Stop saying 'Oh' in that helpless way, and think of something we can do for Roger," said Meade, peering into the oven.

"Well," said Hilma, pulling herself up out of the chair and attempting to rally, "there's always food, and flowers, although that doesn't seem appropriate for a horse that's not quite dead yet."

"Roger said it could be any minute," said Meade. "He has put up a little temporary structure around Squeaky. Apparently the horse can't move, and Roger was worried about him standing out there in the cold."

"A house to die in," said Hilma.

"We are thankful that he is not in pain," said Meade.

"How long can it take a horse to die?" asked Hilma. "Especially a horse like Squeaky, who has lived so very long. If he must wait for his whole life to pass in review, it could be weeks, even months." She pictured Roger growing fat on the endless casseroles and baked hams, and Squeaky standing in his little house, his head drooping lower and lower, re-calling the summer of the terrible horse-flies, the winter of thrush, the other horses that had shared his pasture and then moved on, either to new homes and owners, or to that permanent home on a spot of low ground way back in the woods, dragged out of the pasture by a tractor with a chain around their necks.

"I'm terribly worried about Roger," said Meade. "He's up at five every morning collecting predawn-darkness dew for his yellow nutsedge rust project, he's giving a seminar five evenings a week on peanut diseases, he has his papers to write—and yet he drives out there twice a day to check on Squeaky. Then there's the dread preying on him of what he must do at the first sign of suffering, and on top of it all, this cold weather, his system weakened by stress, and all the germs he is exposed to in those close class-rooms filled with the hot breath of agricul-ture students."

"Damping off," said Hilma irrelevantly, but Meade ignored her and began laying out an elaborate plan: Roger's daily life must be made easier; he must be relieved of all the little household chores—laundry, the preparation of meals, housecleaning tasks. He should come home at night to a bright clean home, a supper warm on the back of the stove, and his bed turned down.

"Oh, Meade," Hilma protested. "I should think now, of all times, Roger might like to be left alone."

"He will be left alone," said Meade. "We will do all these things in the afternoon, when he is at the peanut seminar. Of course we will be gone when he comes home, but his house will have been made comfortable for him."

"Like hovering elves," said Hilma, "always ready to spring into service as soon as his back is turned. I think we would make him nervous and edgy, Meade, never knowing when he will find in the privacy of his own home the work of little unseen hands."

"Roger, nervous and edgy?" said Meade. "Think of all the things Roger has done for you over the years, Hilma; now is your chance to be a help to him for a change. Now you bake a loaf of bread; I will take some sturdy vegetable soup from my freezer. And try to find your little step stool. We will wash the kitchen windows. Nothing should impede the brightness of the morning sun—sunlight is very important to someone in distress."

And so the good work began. Hilma spent the afternoon teetering on the step stool in Roger's azalea bushes, washing the outsides of the windows, while Meade washed the insides, tapping on the glass now and then to point out smudges in the corners that Hilma had missed. They set the table, left the supper dished up on a plate over hot water, and drove home in the dusk.

"When you are feeling sorry for yourself, that is just when you should do something nice for someone else, is what I always say," Meade pronounced. "Now don't you feel better?"

But Hilma just felt a little dizzy, and the tips of her fingers were sore. That night when she pulled back the covers, there was a lizard in her bed, a green anole, stiff and flattened and nearly frozen between the sheets. It didn't seem like a good omen, and she thought of old Squeaky, standing on his four feet in the cold moonlight in his little dying house.

The next day at Roger's house there was a note for them—thanks for the pleasant homecoming—and three containers of stew thawing in the sink, one for Roger's supper, and one each for Hilma and Meade. They swept the kitchen floor, but even Meade did not feel equal to moving on to the other rooms of the house, where papers, folders, and books covered the floors, tables, chairs, and beds in meaningful-looking stacks.

"Well," said Meade, and Hilma sighed with relief. That afternoon she replanted her seeds in the sterilized soil, and that night Roger brought her a vase full of her favorite camellia, 'Magnoliaeflora.'

"I know you don't like the fussy ones," he said.

They talked for a while about Squeaky: Roger said, "We grew up together, and then it seemed like all of a sudden Squeaky was old and I was just middle-aged." About Meade: Hilma said, "She's never easy unless she's taking care of people." And about microscopic animals: Roger said that almost every part of every organism is inhabited by a specific nematode, so that if it were possible for the entire earth and its inhabitants to in-

stantly disappear, leaving only the nematodes, the shape of our world would still
be visible for a few seconds, outlined by
the mass of these invisible creatures.
Then Roger said that he thought this
would be the last freeze, and that in a
couple of weeks it would be safe to plant
her seedlings out. There were no lizards
in the bed, and Hilma lay between her
smooth sheets thinking about the ghost
of a gone world, lingering for one second
in space and then dissolving into the silvery dust of collapsing nematodes.

The next morning she got up early and
drove out to Roger's old home place. Of
course there was no use in it, Meade
would say, but Hilma wanted to see
Squeaky one last time, dying on his four
feet in the little house Roger had built for
him. It wasn't hard to find. The house
was made of slabs of Styrofoam sup-
ported by bamboo poles, and it was a
blaze of white in the gray and tan of the
winter-seared field. It was bigger than
Hilma had expected; four horses could
have died comfortably in this house, she
thought. It had a sloped roof to shed rain,
and one window cut out of the front Styrofoam panel so that Squeaky could see

out over the field and into the longleaf woods beyond. Inside, the ground was covered with wood shavings. There was a bucket of water and a bucket of feed, just in case.

Squeaky was a black horse, grizzled now around the face, gaunt and spare, with big bones and big feet. He had been born to one of Roger's uncle's logging horses.

"Frances," Hilma said to Squeaky.

One day Frances had paused in her job of snaking a big butt log out of the woods to the sawmill, laid her ears back, and given birth to a little black colt.

"Squeaky," said Hilma.

Roger had named the little thing Squeaky because of its squeals and whinnies, but Squeaky had grown up to be a fine horse, patient and almost thoughtful, with the dignity and grace that is so unmistakable in some special horses.

Inside, the house smelled like hay and pine and sweet feed. Squeaky's head drooped and his tail drooped and his eyelids drooped. Hilma didn't dare pat the old horse, he seemed so frail and delicate. He wouldn't lift his head to look at her, but when she put her hand on his muzzle and felt his old bristly lip flap once against her fingers, it seemed like the most generous of good-byes.

The next day was in the seventies. Hilma put her flats of seedlings out on the steps in the sun. On the porch the lizards were scampering. That night she was wakened by gentle plopping sounds, as one by one the blossoms of Roger's camellias turned loose from their stems and hit the floor. Hilma lay in the dark for a while listening for the next flower to fall. Then, suddenly, with the instant clarity that sometimes comes in night thoughts, she realized why Roger had made Squeaky's house so big. It was so that when the old horse finally pitched over, there would be room for him to fall without crashing into the flimsy walls of the house, and his last thought in this world would not be one of panic as the Styrofoam panels and poles of the dying house collapsed on top of him.

18. NEW SUBDIVISION

"They have stuck some kind of bird up on a post at the entrance to their driveway," said Meade.

"A dead bird?" cried Hilma, putting a hand to her throat.

"It's a ceramic bird, I think, or concrete," said Meade. "Some kind of bird of prey, a raptor—perhaps it's meant to be a hawk, although it's bigger than a red-tail."

They were driving out to Tall Pines— "The Finest in Country Living." A group of Wymans—brothers and cousins— had turned their parents' old place into a subdivision with lots marked off, paved roads, a rectangular pond scooped out of what had been a little wet-weather swamp, and streetlamps at regular intervals illuminating the Wymans' old scrubby woods. While the bulldozer tracks were still fresh at the edge of the pond, the Wyman boys began advertising "Lakefront Homesites" in the newspaper, and before long a young couple from Tallahassee had actually bought a lot and built a brick-veneer house there.

At the driveway Meade boldly stopped the car, and they craned their necks to see the bird. It was a cast-concrete eagle, presenting its ruffled chest to passersby, wings outstretched, head to one side.

"Well, I never," said Hilma. "It's an eagle. Imagine an eagle, just sitting there year after year, in that awkward position."

"Pretension is what it is," said Meade.

The next day when Hilma and Meade drove by, there was another post, topped by another eagle. They faced each other across the driveway.

"Two eagles!" cried Hilma. "I have seen pictures in *National Geographic* of a tree full of eagles in one of those wild western states, but it certainly wasn't presented as something you would see every day."

"I think we should call on them," said Meade.

"But our thoughts are not kind," said Hilma, "so our good wishes would be insincere."

"We wouldn't express good wishes," said Meade. "You would bake them a little cake, and we would merely say hello."

A thousand-year-old tree, thought Meade, looking at the redwood siding on the wall under the little porch—and felled for such a house as this.

Everything matches, thought Hilma, noticing the two gleaming brass light fixtures flanking the door and the pair of urns planted with juniper on the top step.

"Oh! Hi!" said the young woman in the doorway. There was a confusion of introductions, then a mingling of gratitude and apology for the cake.

"How nice!"

". . . just a simple banana nut cake."

". . . my favorite, and Bob will be so . . ."

". . . not enough nuts, and my oven, I don't know . . ."

"Won't you come in—Justin, get the

dog, Justin, Justin!" But it was too late. A big black and white dog with a pink nose bounded into the room, over the back of the sofa, and into the kitchen, where it skidded on the linoleum, crashed into the refrigerator, and then started snuffling through the garbage pail. From the yard a little boy called, "Here, boy, here, boy," and Hilma pressed herself up against the redwood wall as the dog dashed back out.

"*101 Dalmatians,*" the woman explained.

"One hundred and one?" gasped Hilma.

"You know how it is with kids," said the woman. "Now come in, I'll take your coats, please sit down." The room was long and low, with pale blue wall-to-wall carpeting and knotty pine paneling. A big plate-glass window looked out into a thicket of myrtle and rows of planted slash pine. The woman flipped a switch on the wall, and the logs in the fireplace instantly burst into flames.

Meade stretched a hand out to the fire, but a glass panel across the fireplace opening prevented any warmth from entering the room.

"We like the rustic look, but we were

concerned about safety, with kids and all," said the woman, "you can never be too careful."

"Oh no," said Hilma, gazing with rapt horror at the logs, wreathed in flames but never consumed, "you can never be too careful with small children."

The door opened just a crack, and the little boy squeezed into the room. A black and white snout appeared for an instant on either side of his legs, then between them as the dog shoved and squirmed to get in.

"Justin," the woman said, in a warning tone.

"We noticed your eagles," said Meade.

"That's how we knew someone lived here," said Hilma hurriedly, "and so we came to say hello."

"Those are exact replicas of the eagles at a certain castle in England," said the woman. "I can't remember the name, but we saw it on 'Masterpiece Theatre.' And believe me, they were *not* cheap."

"What's this?" the little boy called from the kitchen.

"That is some delicious banana nut cake," said the woman in a shrill, cheerful voice, "that these nice ladies have brought us, Justin. Wasn't that nice of them?"

"I hate food with nuts in it," said the little boy, trailing away down a dark hall.

"I have set up a bird-feeding station," said the woman, and she pointed to a cedar bird feeder in the shape of a barn, and a white plastic bird bath. "Now that we live in this wooded area we want Justin to learn to appreciate nature."

"Oh," Hilma began helpfully, forcing her attention away from the mesmerizing fire. "You should be seeing finches, chickadees, chipping sparrows and white-throated sparrows, tufted titmice, and this seems to be a year for the pine siskins."

"Well, I don't know," said the woman. "So far I've only been seeing these little brown birds, and a few black and white ones."

"The floor of the summer house at West Dean Park," Meade said suddenly in a loud voice, "in the southeast of England, is paved entirely with horses' teeth."

Then there were a few awkward moments of silence before Hilma began talking about the weather, "very cold for the time of year," and before long Hilma and Meade gathered up their coats and said good-bye.

On the ride back home Hilma kept thinking of Mr. and Mrs. Wyman, an old county family. "Those were such magnificent woods in the Wymans' day," she said at last. "An open stand of virgin longleaf pines." The Wyman boys had sold the longleaf trees for saw timber in the seventies, when the price was high.

"And now that it's had twenty years to grow up in second-growth loblolly and hardwood thickets, it's called a 'wooded area' by an ignorant fool of a woman who doesn't know a bald eagle from a tufted titmouse," said Meade. " 'A certain castle in England,' " she hissed, " 'little brown birds.' " Meade abhorred imprecision in conversation. "I can only hope that she had her tubes tied after the birth of that child."

"Oh, Meade," said Hilma. "Ignorance is not an inherited trait. But it is a shame about those woods."

"They were such cute little old ladies," the woman said to her husband that night. "One of them was sweet, she brought some kind of bread. The other one was odd, she would just say the strangest things. But they loved the eagles."

"You shouldn't blame the poor little family with the eagles. It's not their fault," said Roger. Although he took his tea plain, he knew that Meade would not stop until she had laid down a cloth and set out the sugar bowl, cream pitcher, spoons, napkins, and cake, and he waited patiently with his hands in his lap. "It's the Wyman boys who should be ashamed, the way they clear-cut those woods. It broke my heart seeing those logs coming out of there, four-hundred-year-old trees some of them, truckload after truckload." Roger's own family place was across the road from Tall Pines. Now it was one of the last fragments of what had once been a vast forest of longleaf pine trees stretching across the Southeast from Virginia to Texas, all cut down and sold for timber to make way for roads, farms, and towns. "Some beautiful boards came out of those trees though," said Roger. " 'The forest that built America,' they call it."

Meade poured tea into his cup

through a little silver gimbaled strainer and sat down with a sigh. "Streetlights, Roger! Paved roads, concrete eagles, surly children, unruly dogs, fires that spring up out of nowhere and put out no heat. What are we coming to in this world, Roger, woods that go unburned, covered with second-growth scrub and idiots?"

But it wasn't a question that could be answered and Roger sipped his tea in silence.

"Remember the Wymans' house?" Meade went on. "A square-hewn dogtrot, 1850s—a fine, simple farmhouse. No pretension there."

"Yes," said Roger, bracing himself for what was sure to come in this well-traveled conversation. "I remember the house."

"Those Wyman boys didn't care enough about it to fix the roof, but they didn't let a month go by without paying that fire insurance premium," said Meade. "And by the time the fire truck got there, it was too late."

"Every board in that house was heart pine," said Roger, "cut off that place. The whole house was made out of kindling wood, Meade, nothing could have stopped that fire."

Meade set her teacup into its saucer with an emphatic click. "Nothing could have stopped it, but what started it," she said, "is what I want to know."

"Now, Meade, you don't—" said Roger.

"Fire insurance!" said Meade. "Insurance money paid for those paved roads, insurance paid for that bulldozer, insurance paid for those shallow people to live their small lives in a place where they have no business to be."

"Oh!" said the woman in the doorway. "How nice to see you—um—"

"It's Hilma," said Hilma.

"Right right right, now I remember, such a pretty name," said the woman, "and where's your friend?"

"Meade!" said Hilma, with a start. "Meade was busy with other things today. But I've brought you a little book that might help you learn the names of your birds."

"Oh, how nice!" said the woman. "*Peterson Field Guides,*" she read.

"Southeastern birds," said Hilma, "Oh, listen," and she paused. "A white-throated sparrow—such a weary little song—here he is; you'll be seeing him on the feeder, this rather large sparrow with the white patch. See the helpful arrows pointing out significant marks."

"Won't you come in?" said the woman. "It's so warm today, I don't think we'll need the fire on, do you?"

"Oh no," said Hilma, "certainly not the fire, not today at all. I can't stay, I just wanted you to have the book. Here," and she opened it to a page of finches, "I have marked the ones you will be likely to see. Your little boy might enjoy making a list."

"You what?" said Meade. "Well, I'm sure it's the only book in that house. I know she didn't offer you anything to eat, we certainly never saw a slice of that banana nut cake."

"I didn't want anything to eat," said Hilma. "I thought she could start with finches and sparrows. Just standing on the porch, I heard a white-throated sparrow."

"With that dog I'm surprised she has any birds at all," said Meade, "except those eagles, of course, bolted to their posts."

It was late in the afternoon, a damp day with an east wind. Roger stood for a minute feeling the wind and the humidity in the air. With a match he lit a little spot in the dry grass beside his raked fire lane, then dribbled a line of fuel oil with his fire torch. With a whoosh the fire swept along the trail of fuel, then leaned with the wind into the woods. Roger stood and watched. The flames burned slow but steady, kept low by the damp air, the wind pushing the line of fire deeper and deeper into the woods. It looked right. Roger walked for over two miles, carefully laying down fire with the torch, stopping from time to time to watch it burn, walking back now and then to be sure the fire had not crossed over his raked path.

When the fire got a few feet out into the woods, it took off. In open areas, where the big trees were thin, the accumulation of straw was sparse, and the fire burned slow and close to the ground. There had been a good seedfall the year before, and the little longleaf seedlings spread out a cool place with their green needles to protect themselves from the fire. But where the big old trees were thick and filled up the sky with their tops, there was no opening for the little seedlings. There the pine straw lay thick on the ground, a volatile fuel, and in those places the flames licked up into the sky ten feet or more. Smoke rose in towering bulbs, there was a roaring sound, and the tops of the trees swayed and danced in the fire's wind. As many times as he had done this job, Roger still worried. It was a delicate business, balancing fire, fuel, wind, and water. Many times he stopped and watched and worried. But every time the hot spots burned through quickly, the flames sank down again, and the fire crept deeper and deeper into the woods. By midnight he had lit off the whole thing, and he just stood and watched it burn. Behind the flames the ground looked bare, black, and ashy, but it would rain tomorrow, and by the middle of next week blades of grass would begin to show, and in the spring the wire grass, bracken fern, and all the other fire-dependent ground covers of the longleaf pine woods would come up lush and green and sturdy, rejuvenated by this fire. By April only the sooty trunks of the great old trees would show that these woods had burned. Maybe needles on some lower limbs would be browned, Roger thought, peering up into the smoky sky—but maybe not. It was a good fire.

"A forest fire!" the woman said to Hilma, gazing despondently out her window at Roger's blackened woods. "We could have lost our home!"

"No," said Hilma, trying to explain, "it wasn't that kind—"

"You should have seen the flames!" said the woman.

"But these woods need fire to keep them healthy. It's—"

"I just kept thinking over and over: 'Only You Can Prevent Forest Fires, Only You Can Prevent Forest Fires.' I called 911, I called the fire department. But no one came!"

"But," Hilma persisted, "it's the exclusion of fire, the suppression of fire, that would be dangerous and bad—"

"Just look at my view!" the woman

wailed, and burst into tears, flailing her arms at the window.

"Gone?" said Hilma.

"Both of them," smacked Meade. "Just the posts are left." It was a warm day in March and Meade had taken a drive out to Tall Pines.

"Meade, you didn't—" said Hilma.

"Hilma!" said Meade. "What can you be thinking? Ask her yourself next time you go out there to give her a little lesson in fire ecology."

"I don't know," said the woman. "I just don't know."

In the front yard, pieces of the eagles were strewn around their posts: the fan of a tail, a section of ruffled chest, a hooked beak, a glowering eye, crunched and smattered. The bird feeder was empty, and on the steps the two junipers in their matching urns had died perfectly symmetrically, from the bottom up. In the house the curtains were drawn closed, the blue wall-to-wall carpet was tracked up with mud, and on the sofa in the room with the picture window the little boy lay, slathered with pink calamine lotion, watching cartoons with drooping eyes. The woman wandered aimlessly around and around the room, touching her forehead gently every now and then with her fingertips.

"Try to look at the bright side," said Hilma. "Maybe the eagles weren't quite right for here anyway. Maybe they were a little bit . . ."

"Those were five-hundred-dollar eagles," the woman said in a pinched, even voice, "exact replicas. . . ." But she began to sob, and couldn't finish. "I feel so lonely here, and frightened—I thought we would have neighbors, but there's no one but us, then the forest fire, now vandals, this poison ivy, and yesterday that snake on the steps. I don't know, I just don't know."

"But it was only a white oak snake," said Hilma. "It's not as if a cottonmouth moccasin had—"

"I don't want to learn the names of snakes!" the woman sputtered, clutching her head with both hands, and Hilma thought it best not to mention that with warmer weather, moccasins would begin to stir at the swampy edge of the rectangular lake, where button bushes had begun to grow again, hiding the tracks of the bulldozers.

Meade stopped the car at the entrance to the driveway. " 'For Sale,' " she read triumphantly. "The Finest in Country Living was not good enough for them."

"Poor little thing," said Hilma. "I wonder if she ever learned her sparrows."

In the front yard the shards of eagle had been cleaned up, but the octagonal concrete posts had been left at the entrance to the driveway, and a pair of eagle feet still clutched the top of each post with menacing talons.

19. LOOKING FOR PEROTE

It was in the middle of the February meeting of the writers' group that Hilma spotted the dead rat. She had set the trap the night before in a dark corner of the room, but the fury of the snap must have catapulted the trap, for now it lay at some distance from the wall, right in the path from this dining table to the kitchen.

"I will get more hot water," said Lucy, looking into the teapot and beginning to rise.

"Oh no, you sit there, I will . . ." said Hilma, almost leaping from her chair.

Luckily, all eyes were on Beulah Hambleton, who was explaining the latest installment in her detective thriller. "It will all become clear at the end, you see—it was a scratch from a poisoned pin that did him in."

It would be so easy, Hilma thought, on the way to the kitchen with the teapot, to just . . . But when she reached the rat she couldn't bring herself to stoop and pick it up. Even with Beulah Hambleton in the middle of *Murder from Scratch,* someone's attention might wander. That new member perhaps, Heather Bell, a young technician Lucy had brought from the experiment station; with her powers of observation honed by science, she would be the one most likely to notice the rat. The way she peered out from behind those two sheaves of hair and never smiled or spoke—who could tell what she saw and what she thought about it? A nicely furnished room, a little cluttered perhaps, but cozy, a stream of late winter light filtering through the lace curtains, and an old woman in a rump-sprung wool skirt walking to the kitchen, a Blue Willow teapot in one hand and a dead rat dangling from a trap in the other.

So the rat lay, right through Mary Bell Geeter's family history detailing the union of two prominent families, the Georgia Geeters and the Alabama Thrashes, and on into a discussion of the annual writers' group picnic.

In spite of being stone dead, Hilma noticed, the rat had quite an alert, almost expectant expression, its little bright eyes thrust wide open by the blow, its little gnarly front feet clutching the corners of the trap.

"There is Mrs. Malcolm's lovely house and garden, out on old 19," someone was saying. "A nice setting for a picnic, although she does have all those pets; that weasel-like creature that smells so bad and those big yellow dogs that . . ."

It was clever the way the red capital V for Victor outlined the head of the rat in the caught position; although really, Hilma thought, Victor was much too strong a word for such a small death.

". . . birdseed flung all over the carpet, and then the MICE of course . . ."

Little inverted serifs at the top of the V formed the two ears of the rat, and two little red dots for . . . The eyes are the windows to the soul—that is true, Hilma thought. It is hard to tell what someone is thinking when you can't see the eyes.

At this very moment, for example, Heather Bell might be watching, her eyes hidden in the shadows of hair, and thinking—

"—Roger's old home place, Hilma?"

"Hilma?"

And suddenly all around the table her guests were straining forward in their chairs, watching her and waiting, their eyes alert and expectant, their knuckly fingers clutching their teacups.

"Roger?" yelped Hilma.

"It was a John Wind house, one of his finest," said Mary Bell Geeter, "circa 1840, originally very similar to the Mash house; the porches were added."

"The picnic, at Roger's old home place?" said Hilma, feeling very vague. "But there's no house there—just the chimney."

"But we were saying, Hilma, that it should be different this year, after this bitter cold winter. We should have a real picnic, outdoors, to celebrate spring," Lucy explained patiently.

"Such a gorgeous setting, and so much history there, the ancient avenue of oaks, the hill, and that chimney rearing up against the sky," said Lucille

Sanders, who was writing a romance story.

"What about toilets?" said Heather Bell. There was an embarrassed pause as people came to grips with this suggestion, and then everyone began talking all at once about rain.

"Rain!"

"We must think about rain of course!"

"We must plan in case of rain!"

"We will have portable toilets," said Lucy, "and tents set up on the hill. There will be room for everyone to take refuge in case of rain. The next step is to talk to Roger, and if Hilma would . . ." Once again the bright eyes turned to Hilma, then the writers' meeting was over and helpful guests began gathering up dishes.

"Oh no!" said Hilma. "Don't bother! I'll clear all this away!" There were last-minute trips to the bathroom, and Hilma waited with dread for the horrified cry. But it never came, and finally everyone stood at the door sorting out their coats and saying good-bye.

"The tents could go here on this flat place," said Lucy, pacing off a distance.

"And the toilet off there, behind the sasanquas." Roger was poking around the base of the chimney with a stick, worried that the tramp of so many feet might loosen the foundation and bring it tumbling down at last, and Hilma was standing at the top of the hill, looking off toward Perote.

"What do you think, Roger," asked Lucy, "Port-O-Lets where your grandmother's formal garden used to be, and people trooping around up here, eating congealed salads off of paper plates?"

"There were guests here when there was a house. Why shouldn't there be guests now that the house is gone?" said Roger.

"It's like gold that has been passed through fire to purge it of its dross," said Lucy. She stood looking off into the open pine woods, where the dogwoods and plum trees were in full bloom. "It feels like hallowed ground."

At least there would be a nobler race of rats here, Hilma thought, filled with the health and vigor of the great outdoors, foraging for their own food and making nests out of twigs and sweet grass—not nasty, nearsighted town-dwelling rats, scuttling inside walls, scavenging and scrounging and at last lying dead and undiscovered in traps with their eyes wide open.

But suddenly Lucy and Roger were asking her something about acid soil and columbines.

"... Hilma?"

"Columbine?" said Hilma.

"The lime leaching out of the mortar might sweeten the soil in that spot," said Lucy, and then Hilma saw the little columbine growing up by the chimney.

The next writers' group meeting was held at Heather Bell's apartment, all white Sheetrock and high-gloss polyurethane. No danger of coming up on a little unexpected death here, Hilma thought, although she had been startled by a black and white photograph on the cover of a magazine in the bathroom showing a woman wearing a very short black skirt and over-the-knee black socks, sprawled across the curb of a busy city street as if she had tripped over her own thick-soled, high-heeled shoes. She was lying there, propped up on her elbows, glaring at something or someone unseen off to one side with angry eyes, her dark black lips screwed up in some kind of taunt or insult. Maybe someone had pushed her.

". . . and there, in the garden, cushioned on a bed of Spanish moss, safe in his encircling arms—" Lucille Sanders was reading with feeling, a little quaver in her voice.

But someone cried, "Chiggers!" and two or three more people said, "They would be covered with chiggers!" and then everyone was talking all at once about chiggers and Spanish moss.

What had made that woman so angry, Hilma wondered, and who was she shouting at, and why did she keep lying there stretched across the curb in that awkward position, her feet weighted down and almost bent backward by the cruel black shoes?

". . . funeral tents and one portable toilet. Roger says the 'Lady Banksia' will be in full bloom."

And with such a photograph in her bathroom, what must Heather Bell think of them all with their teapots and their "Lady Banksia," their Georgia Geeters and their Alabama Thrashes, and their heroes' encircling arms? Hilma wondered.

". . . and if it is a clear day, we will be able to see all the way to Perote," said Lucy.

Roger was right—the 'Lady Banksia' was in full bloom, a spectacular column of roses twining up a pine tree in what had been the front garden. Every now and then a breeze would send a shower of yellow petals down over the writers' group picnic. It was the middle of pine pollen season too, and when the wind blew a certain way, a shimmering yellow haze could be seen drifting in the air, and every surface was coated with a layer of golden dust.

Crumbling rows of bricks outlined the foundation of the house, and several of the older members were standing on the grassy floor of a front room, gazing through imaginary windows into the hazy distance. Every now and then someone would kick up a bit of china or glass, and little groups would form to try to match its pattern and edge to another piece that had been kicked up earlier.

Lucille Sanders was strolling with Roger along the mossy brick pathways of the old garden, describing to him her idea for her next year's writing project, a sort of romantic gardener's journal—"not about digging in the dirt," she said, "but about the emotions inspired by a garden."

"Oh," said Roger.

"Take these daffodils, for example," she said, "these dear bulbs thrusting themselves up spring after spring, showing us the patterns of the old garden in which they were planted so many years ago—what memories these bulbs must have, Roger!"

"Well," said Roger, but he did not have the heart to tell Lucille Sanders on this spring day, with her muse so lively, that these were "King Alfred" daffodils, and that he had bought the bulbs down at Gramling's and planted them himself in November 1995.

"You must always start with the death and work backward from there," Beulah Hambleton said to Lucy, shading her eyes and peering up at the elegant corbeling at the top of the chimney. "Last year it was the poisoned pin, but this year I feel I want something more violent. I'm always on the lookout for new deaths."

"Samuel Meadows, Roger's great-great-great-grandfather, is said to have planted these live oaks." Mary Bell Geeter was picking thrips out of the punch with a long-handled spoon and giving a lesson in local history to several people who stood under the funeral tent, patiently holding out their little glass cups. "But they were *actually* planted by my distant cousin, the same Harriet Thrash Geeter who brought the first 'Chandleri Elegans' to Georgia from Screamer, Alabama."

Hilma was taking a little walk down the hill in the shade of the oak trees and thinking about bits of a conversation she had overheard outside the Port-O-Let:

"Is Hilma getting—"

"Or is she just a little—"

"So often she seems to be off in—"

"And at her age to be—"

But it wasn't that, Hilma thought. There was nothing wrong with her mind. It was just that sometimes she couldn't stop thinking about certain things that got her attention; and it is perfectly natural, after all, for the human mind to cling to things that interest it, like chiggers on Spanish moss.

Then, around a bend in the road she

saw Heather Bell, sitting on a kind of seat formed by a loop of grapevine twining up a tree trunk. Hilma was afraid of Heather Bell—her dark gaze, her gloomy silence, and that troubling photograph in the bathroom. But something about seeing her in that vulnerable position, dangling from a tree, her feet not quite touching the ground, made Hilma feel able to approach her quite boldly.

"What a nice seat you have found," she said.

"Here," said Heather Bell, shifting over to make room. "You can sit down too." When she smiled and pushed her hair behind her ears, Hilma could see that she really had a pleasant face, with a generous jaw and appealing-looking crooked teeth.

It was a surprisingly pleasant seat, springy and ample, with the trunk of the vine forming a backrest. "Why," said Hilma, swinging her feet happily, "I feel that my mind could almost soar in this spot."

"This is a beautiful place," said Heather Bell.

"And how nice a home is when there is no house there," said Hilma.

They dangled together for a few minutes, quite companionably. Then Heather Bell asked, "What is it they are all looking for up there on the hill?"

"Oh," said Hilma, "years ago there was a town over there, miles away, and on a clear day it was said that from the upstairs windows of this house you could see the white buildings of Perote. Now, of course, the house is gone, and the town is gone too, just a crossroads and a few mobile homes."

"But people still look for it?" asked Heather Bell.

"Oh yes," said Hilma, "on clear days like this, a few people still look for Perote."

20. IMPASSIONED TYPOGRAPHER II

"He's cooking the rabbits that ate the R out of RIGHT HERE," said Eula. "That's what you smell." It was a warm day, the kitchen windows were open, and from Louise's house next door the smells of thyme and garlic and meat slowly cooking in wine wafted across two side yards and part of a garden.

"He's a good cook," said Ethel, "I'll say that for him. I just hope they don't both get tularemia and die."

"I just hope he doesn't accidentally shoot himself—or you or Louise either, Eula," said Lucy. "He probably never held a gun in his life before this." They were talking about the typographer from Kansas City, who had stayed on and on and on at Louise's house after his wife had left in a huff, wearing strange clothes and behaving oddly. At first Louise had visited him shyly, taking little gifts of letters and numbers, but then she had begun helping him with his assemblages, putting together collections of wood and metal and plastic junk mixed in with random letters and bits of phrases from roadside signs. Gradually Louise had moved back into her house, and now, in the spring of the year, there they were, Louise and the typographer, living together quite cozily, cooking, eating, working, and shooting rabbits, happy and content in a way that nobody could quite understand.

"Louise did the shooting," said Eula. "He was sleeping out there to keep the rabbits out, between the R and the I, flat on his back on the bare ground, every night, drenched with dew, then the rabbits came in when they were gone hunting for letters on the road, and ate the tail off that R, and Louise got out the gun and shot two of them."

In the middle of Louise's garden, the typographer had flattened a section of raised beds and he and Louise had sown garden cress to spell out the words RIGHT HERE in capital letters. Beyond the words, in an undisturbed raised bed, the numbers 0 to 9 in rye grass ran west to east.

"What does it mean," asked Lucy, " 'RIGHT HERE 023456789'?"

"Oh, you know Louise," said Eula. "She thinks the time is right, spring, and something about this full moon and the letters and numbers, the spacemen are coming down this week, she says."

"And what about him?" said Ethel. "Is he waiting for the spacemen too?"

"Oh, him—spacemen wouldn't surprise him. When we were skinning those rabbits, that man told me . . ." said Eula, and she put down a bowl of beans on the table and beckoned Lucy and Ethel to the window, where they leaned against the sink and looked out into Louise's garden. "Skinning those rabbits, he told me where he used to work at his last job the rabbits all wore clothes! Little outfits! Shoes! Hats! Little blue coats!"

"Hallmark cards," said Lucy.

"Oh," said Eula. "Well, he don't care about the spacemen, any more than he cared about that wife that left him and flew back to Kansas City. He's just in it for the letters."

"Look at Tom out there trying to talk redneck to him," said Ethel. The typographer was watching Louise fasten a rusty piece of corrugated metal to a panel of hog wire, and Tom was standing back, slouching a little and looking grim and uncomfortable.

"Tom's worried about Louise," said Eula. "He thinks the typographer is up to something—raping, strangling, stealing, although I don't see that in him." They all three shifted a little closer and peered out the window at the typographer. He was wearing purple short pants with a drawstring waist and a big shirt with giant red and mauve flowers all over it. His toes grappled over the edge of his pink shower shoes.

"Why does Tom wear that cap?" said Ethel. "It's deforming his head."

"How you doing?" said Tom, nodding and touching the brim of his cap. But he didn't smile, and his jaws were tight.

"Hi there!" said the typographer. He was holding a red-and-white-striped scrap of board from a railroad-crossing sign in one hand and a piece of galvanized guttering in the other. Louise was squatting down, carefully attaching black letters printed on clear plastic along one edge of the hog wire.

"Tom," she said, "there's not gon' be chairs enough for them."

"Name's Tom," said Tom, reaching over Louise to shake hands with the typographer. "I was raised right over there next door. Louise is my aunt."

"Tom," said Louise, "the fields is gon' be glittering with their eyes." She took off a capital F and replaced it with an H. She twisted an R and straightened an M. No matter how you read it, the letters didn't spell anything. The typographer stood back and shook his head.

"Look at that," he said. "It's all in the juxtaposition, that's the key. Man, she's got the touch."

Tom paced around Eula's kitchen, picking things up off the counter and then putting them back down, glowering out from under the brim of his Feed Rite cap.

"It ain't right," he said, and Eula sighed and began putting food down on the table. "The man is a nut. He's worse than Louise! 'The touch,' he says, yeah, right, he ought to know—he's touched worse than Louise, touched in the head!"

"Oh, Tom," said Eula, arranging the handles of the serving spoons so that they aimed at Tom, "everybody's a little crazy if you get to know them good enough. Take Roger's little girlfriend Della, always pacing around with that gone look in her eyes, yet a perfectly nice woman, and knows her birds. Your own daddy, my Melvin, much as I loved him, I wouldn't say he wasn't crazy on the subject of fighting cocks. Why, look at Ethel—"

"Whoa, Aunt Eula," said Ethel.

"Everybody's got that little side to them, Tom, it's just some of them you see it sooner. He ain't no worse than most."

"It ain't right," said Tom, glaring across the butter beans at Ethel. "Your own mama, Ethel, living in that house with a lunatic. You could go over there one morning and find her raped and strangled."

"And we would never know whether it was the spacemen or the typographer that did it," said Ethel, "would we, Tom?"

"The Bible says you're supposed to honor your father and mother, Ethel, you're supposed to take care of them when they get old and feeble. You're not supposed to sit back and look on while some nut from the Wild West moves in and eggs her on to be crazier than she already is. You don't know what his intentions are, why he's there, how long he's going to stay. Hell, I don't even think he's paying her any rent!"

"I am taking care of her, Tom," said Ethel. "I'm leaving her alone."

But that afternoon when Tom had gone back to marking trees and the typographer had driven off in his van ("Grocery store," said Eula, "you watch, he'll come back with three bags"), Lucy and Ethel went over to Louise's house.

"How long is he going to stay, Louise?" asked Lucy in a loud voice.

"5:35 a.m. in the morning, Lucy, is when they're coming. We calculated it with an alarm clock," said Louise, and on the scrubbed kitchen table she lined up three early peas and turned the salt-shaker on its side. "Ethel, honey, you ought to come home for this."

But Ethel was poking around in a container of rabbit stew in the refrigerator. The kitchen had a clean lemony smell. "Look at this—" Ethel stood back and gazed deep into the refrigerator. "No moldy beans, no withered Fig Newtons, no rotten milk. Did the spacemen clean out this icebox, Mama?"

Louise flinched and sucked in her breath. "Don't say that, Ethel!" she snapped. "You don't talk like that! They could hear you, change their plans! You know you can't trust these new clocks from Wal-Mart. Sometimes they tell you the time is right, sometimes they tell you the time is wrong."

"Just tell us one thing, Mama," said Ethel. "Who cleaned out this icebox? It wasn't you, so who was it?"

"Oh," said Louise, "that was him. He does all that in his spare time."

"How long is he going to stay, Louise?" Lucy asked again.

"5:35 a.m., tomorrow morning, they'll swarm through this house like fire ants, through the cracks in the doors and windows they'll come in like mist, their little hands and feet will be all over everything."

The next afternoon Roger stopped by to see Eula on his way home from work. She was standing at the sink, looking out into Louise's garden in the dusk.

"How is she?" asked Roger. "5:35 came and went this morning. I thought about her on my way to the methyl bromide alternatives meeting in Morven."

"Fine," said Eula. "These things slip away from her, Roger. Next thing you know, she'll have out that alarm clock and have figured out another time. That man keeps her busy, he's all the time got her out there putting junk together, keeps her mind off it somewhat, and keeps her from wandering off, although Tom doesn't trust him, thinks he's up to something." Eula leaned up against the sink, wiping her hands over and over with the dish towel. "See that car? There's another man over there now, talking to him, you can see them over there by the RIGHT HERE, although Louise has let that go, you can't hardly read it with the nut grass coming up between the letters." A tall man in a suit was looking at the arrangements of junk the typographer and Louise had wired and welded and stapled together. Some of them were lying on the ground. Some were propped up against the chicken-yard fence. Every now and then the man would step back and look at something from a distance or step closer and peer at a letter or a word or a piece of rusty metal as if he expected to be able to read it.

"Tom doesn't trust him, thinks he's up to something. But you know Tom, he always looks for the worst. Now Tom's mad at Ethel, because she won't take Louise in to live with her, and Ethel's mad at Tom because it ain't really his business, and Tom thinks I'm taking Ethel's side, and, oh, I don't know." Eula flapped the dish towel in the air. "Just between you and me, Roger, I think she's better off living with a lunatic and a houseful of spacemen than with Ethel, every room filled up with boats, and Ethel like she is, with the men—oh, Roger, I shouldn't have said . . . oh, Roger," and she buried her face in the dish towel.

But Roger said, "It's all right to say that to me, Eula," and Eula folded the dish towel into threes and went on. "And here I am, in the middle of it, dodging here and there, trying to keep the peace, worrying about Louise, I feel like I'm skating on the rink of disaster, Roger. Lucy's doing her best, she was over there trying to talk to Louise, but you can't find out anything from Louise, it's just spacemen, spacemen, spacemen. Roger, sit down and have a cup of coffee."

"Why don't you try to talk to him?" said Roger.

"Him?" said Eula.

"They don't understand what you're doing here," said Roger to the typographer. "And they're worried about Louise. She's hard to reason with because of the spacemen, and they worry about her."

"Reason with?" said the typographer. "Reason?" He pulled out a black capital track-sign R from a stack of letters and numbers. "If 'reason' is a rut, then she is the rising sun," he said, holding up the R in front of Roger with both hands. "If 'reason' is a rat, then she is a white rhinoceros. If 'reason' is a roach, then she is a raptor. That woman has moved so far beyond 'reason,' it's— You want to know what I think of 'reason'?" he said, and he flipped the R and laid it down beside a splintered piece of drip-cap molding, upside down and backward. It was printed on clear plastic, so it read from both sides. "There," said the typographer, stepping back and looking hard at Roger. "She taught me that. 'Juxtaposition,' that one word, that is the key. She taught me that, and, man, I was in the right place at the right time, and I don't mean here—" He spread his arms at the garden and the two houses and the stretch of road and the field across the road, where the corn was just beginning to tassel. "I mean here," and he tapped his head. "At last, somebody is looking after me." He threw his head back and held his hands up to the sky. "Thank you, little spacemen, thank you!"

Eula and Ethel and Lucy stood in a row at Eula's kitchen sink and looked out the window. The panels of hog wire, the bedsprings, the piles of letters and numbers and words, and the assemblages were gone.

"He's gone," said Eula. "Roger went over there and talked to him, and the next thing we knew, he was gone."

"Where's Louise?" asked Lucy.

"Oh, Louise is right back doing her regular doings," said Eula, "lining up her letters, winding up that alarm clock, talking about the little hands and feet, you know Louise."

"Not raped and strangled?" said Ethel.

"Oh, that was just Tom, all that raping and strangling talk," said Eula.

"Tom!" shouted Ethel. "Where are you? I was right and you were wrong, Tom!"

"What did Roger say to him?" asked Lucy.

"Roger just got him to talking," said Eula. "Seems like that man we saw here in the rented car wanted to have an art show, just our typographer's artwork, in Kansas City, says Roger, a something, a juxtaposition of his work, something."

"A retrospective," said Lucy.

"That's it," said Eula. "So next thing we knew, he had it loaded up in that van, and him and all of it gone back to Kansas City."

They stood together at the sink and looked out the window at Louise's garden. Nutsedge had obliterated the commanding RIGHT HERE, with its sharp, bold serifs, the rye grass was withering in the late spring heat, blurring the 023456789, and the remaining raised beds were billowing mounds of blue-green grass.

"Look at that," said Eula. "It's just a shame the way Louise has let that garden go." She sighed. "Once that Bermuda grass gets away from you, there's almost nothing you can do."

21. ONION SANDWICH

"Get Roger to do it," said Dr. Vanlandingham, and immediately heads nodded all around the table and the meeting moved on to more important business: planning for next month's Ag Showcase. When Roger got back from the Georgia Peanut Growers meeting in Eufala a week later, an oil painting of an onion sandwich was in his office leaning up against the wall on the floor behind his desk.

"I don't know, Roger," his secretary said. "Dr. Vanlandingham left it here, said you would know what to do with it."

The sandwich was on white bread, thick-cut slabs of white onion, with blobs of something nearly white glistening around the edges. Roger and Mrs. Eldridge stood and looked at it for a minute.

"That has to be mayonnaise," said Mrs. Eldridge.

"It must be a Vidalia onion," said Roger. "Otherwise nobody could eat that much onion in a sandwich."

"It is a Vidalia onion," said Mrs. Eldridge. "That's what the problem is."

"What is the problem?" asked Roger.

"You'll have to ask Dr. Vanlandingham," said Mrs. Eldridge. "All I know is, it's a Vidalia onion sandwich, and that's the problem."

"We are not hanging that painting in the Vidalia Onion Storage Lab," said Dr. Vanlandingham emphatically. "This is a scientific institution, not an art gallery. With your experience, Roger, we thought you would be the best one to deal with it."

"I don't have any experience with onions," said Roger. "I should think Alex Montgomery or Auburn Brown would be the ones—"

"Your experience with women, we

mean," said Dr. Vanlandingham impatiently. "We decided you should be the one to return it to her and explain tactfully how unsuitable it would be to hang a picture like that in a controlled-atmosphere storage laboratory.

"Why can't you hang it somewhere else, where Dr. Vanlandingham won't be offended by the frivolity?" said Lucy. "On the wall of an office, or in a reception area."

"That's the problem," said Roger. "Mrs. Johnson's husband was one of the early Vidalia onion growers; he made a fortune in onions, and left nearly a million dollars to the storage lab. His wife painted it herself and presented it specifically to hang there in his memory."

"It's a terrible painting," said Della, backing away from it with distaste.

"There's definitely something wrong with the mayonnaise," said Lucy. "It looks almost curdled, as if she added the oil too quickly."

"I don't know anything about mayonnaise," said Della. "It's just a terrible painting. I don't blame Dr. Vanlandingham."

"But I like the idea of it," said Roger. "A portrait of a sandwich."

"Why, Dr. Meadows!" Mrs. Johnson greeted Roger at the door. "My husband used to talk about you. What was it—tobacco, soybeans . . ."

"Peanuts," said Roger, "but we all knew Mr. Johnson there at the experiment station. We are all so sorry—" But Mrs. Johnson began to welcome him in a flustered way, almost snatching his hat off his head and bustling him into the next room, where she plumped up sofa cushions and straightened little things on the table. Then she disappeared into the kitchen and began rattling ice cubes and calling out questions about tea, lemon, and sugar in a voice so cheerful it was almost shrill.

The room was very bright. A plate-glass window looked out on an elaborate bird-feeding station, with a little fountain of spray, flagstones interplanted with maidenhair fern, and a clipped hedge of red-tipped photinia so tall and thick you would never know Madison Drive was just on the other side of it. It all looked very cool and peaceful, like a picture in a magazine. Roger felt uneasy about leaning back on the pale, shimmery pillows with their silky tassels, so he sat up on the edge of the sofa trying to keep both feet off the white rug. He tried again:

"Everyone at the experiment station is so sorry about your husband, Mrs. Johnson, and—" But Mrs. Johnson began pouring tea from a yellow pitcher nervously, filling one glass half full and then pouring a little bit into the other glass, and then going back and forth between the two of them as if she couldn't quite make up her mind. A splash of tea slopped onto the rug, but Roger got it quickly with his handkerchief. If she wouldn't even listen to the condolences, he wondered, how in the world was he going to get around to the return of the onion sandwich?

"Mrs. Johnson," he said.

"I've just been painting all these sandwiches," Mrs. Johnson said gaily. "I can't help it. I just keep painting and painting." The walls of the room were lined with paintings of sandwiches in pale frames. The paint looked thick, almost as if it had been daubed on with the back of a spoon, which made the sandwiches appear dry and inedible. There was a tomato sandwich, a cucumber sandwich, a Bibb lettuce sandwich, and what Roger took at first to be a worm sandwich, but on looking more closely, he saw that the worms were clumsily painted bean sprouts.

"I'm running out of sandwiches!" said Mrs. Johnson.

And Roger sprang in: "That Vidalia onion sandwich," he said, "that you gave Dr. Vanlandingham for the lab—we want to thank you, but—"

"I mean, a grilled eggplant sandwich, OK, with some arugula sticking out around the edges," said Mrs. Johnson. "But who ever heard of a squash sandwich? Who ever heard of an okra sandwich?" Even though neither of them had drunk a sip of tea, she began making dashes at the tall, full glasses with the yellow pitcher, and Roger gave up.

He moved an enormous Menoboni bird book off the table onto the white rug, he took the pitcher out of Mrs. Johnson's hands and put it back on the tray, and then he slid the whole thing over to the other side of the table, out of reach. "Mrs.

Johnson," he said, leaning forward earnestly with his elbows on his knees, "please sit still and let me say this to you."

And as if she had been stricken, Mrs. Johnson did sit still, bolt upright in the light blue tufted upholstered chair and stared at Roger with a frightened look. He could see little dimples forming in her chin, and suddenly he remembered Mr. Johnson's big blunt hands, with the tufts of bristly hair on the knuckles, and how he would stand too close in a way that felt intimate and threatening all at the same time and say, "Lemme tell you the one about . . ."

"A controlled atmosphere storage lab is not . . ." and "The director of the lab feels . . ." and "A portrait of an onion sandwich, while it might be . . ." Every one of his carefully rehearsed phrases flew out of his head, and he sat and stared through the glass top of the table at Mrs. Johnson's tense, dry-looking feet. All the strings in the tops of them were stretched tight, as if she might be about to shuck off her thin gold shoes and make a mad dash for safety. The silence seemed strange in that bright room, which she had managed to fill so successfully with noise, and for no reason at all, Roger thought of the little squirming legs of a fat toad-frog on its back in plowed dirt, where Mr. Johnson, touring the onion germ plasm plot, had tossed it right in front of the blades of a disk harrow.

Then Mrs. Johnson said, "My husband was not a nice man, Dr. Meadows. I don't know if you knew that or not."

Experience with women, Roger thought, has gotten me into this. But he told the truth. "Yes, Mrs. Johnson," he said. "Everybody knew that."

"It always seemed odd to me that he became famous for such a mild, bland onion," said Mrs. Johnson.

"The 'Georgia Sweet Onion King,'" said Roger. "No, it didn't fit him."

"It hardly ever makes sense what people do," said Mrs. Johnson. "Look at me: here I am with all this onion money. I could go out of this house right now, go down to Thomasville to Mason's Antiques and buy that little desk he's got in there for twelve thousand dollars, then I could go right over to Travel Time and buy a ticket on a cruise ship to Scandinavia, four meals a day, all summer long, and when I came back I'd have more money in the bank than when I left home. But what do I do? I sit in this house all day and paint these goddamned sandwiches."

"What's wrong with that?" said Roger. "Why should you buy a twelve-thousand-dollar desk and eat four meals a day in Norway if you'd rather be here painting pictures of sandwiches?"

"Well, just look at them!" said Mrs. Johnson, and she flung herself around in her chair and glared back at the pictures. "Just look at these terrible sandwiches! Who could eat a sandwich like that?"

"But," said Roger, "pictures aren't always supposed to be . . . I mean, if you enjoy it, why—"

"Enjoy it?" said Mrs. Johnson, and she stood up out of the blue chair. "Enjoy it?" She glared down at Roger. "I hate painting these sandwiches!" She leaned slightly forward from the waist and covered her mouth with both hands, so that for an instant Roger thought she was going to throw up on the white rug, but instead she burst into tears and just stood there on her tense, tight-strung feet, sobbing and sobbing.

For just a minute Roger felt a flurry of exasperation with Dr. Vanlandingham for his high-minded notions about frivolity in the Vidalia Onion Storage Lab. But then he recovered himself. Nothing could have prepared him to deal with this very strange unhappiness, expressed in oil paintings of gloomy sandwiches, but the one thing he did know for sure was that this room was not suitable for such grief, with its silky fringes, its polished woods, its Boehm porcelain camellias under glass domes; and he took Mrs. Johnson by both shoulders and led her out the French doors and down the steps to the birdbath, where they stood knee-deep in maiden-hair ferns. There was a flurrying exodus of birds. A tufted titmouse hit the plate-glass window with a pop and fell to the ground, where it sat a little lopsided in the liriope, trying to regain its bearings. Roger's pants were soaked up to the knee by the little misting sprayer, but he didn't see how he could move Mrs. Johnson, so he just stood there while she sobbed into his tea-stained handkerchief, patting her on the back from time to time and watching the water fill up her little gold shoes.

22. THE SILVER THREAD

No one could get Meade to understand what an honor it was that Roger had been asked to play the banjo on the Old Marble Stage at the Florida Folk Festival in May. It was the oldest and largest music festival of its kind in the U.S. This year an estimated thirty thousand people would gather on the banks of the Suwannee River to commemorate Florida's musical heritage.

"Riffraff!" said Meade. "They will all be wearing halter tops and eating cotton candy."

"You can't keep thirty thousand people from doing that, Meade," said Hilma.

"Just try to ignore the people and concentrate on the music," said Lucy. "Gamble Rogers, Doc Watson, and Vassar Clements have all played at the Florida Folk Festival. Will McLean played 'Hold Back the Waters of Lake Okeechobee' on the very same spot where Roger will stand."

But still, Meade didn't like the sound of it. The whole state of Florida seemed like nothing more than a glorified sandbar to her, barely above sea level, and what good there used to be of it now ruined by development. "But Roger is not from Florida!" she kept saying. "And he's not 'folk'!"

"Still," said Hilma, "surely you will come with Lucy and me and sit on a blanket on the side of the hill in the May Florida sunset and see Roger down there on the stage singing and playing for all those people."

"Why?" said Meade. "When I can sit in the comfort of my own living room and have Roger sit in the Windsor chair without arms and play 'Trouble in Mind' anytime I like, and then have a nice visit afterwards, with something good to eat—why should I sit on the hard ground in the hot sun breathing the bug spray of thirty thousand Floridians, Roger a tiny speck in the distance. From that far away you probably can't even make out the words."

"There is a sophisticated amplification system," said Lucy. "You'll be able to hear every note."

"And besides," said Hilma, "think of Roger. I'm sure it would reassure him to know that you were sitting somewhere out there on the hard ground with the riffraff, listening to his performance."

"Oh," said Meade, "well."

"I don't know if I'm gon' be able to stand it, Roger," Eula called to Roger, who was up in the middle of her plum tree, pruning out dead limbs with a chain saw. "Seeing you up there on that marble stage in front of all those people, singing those same songs Melvin used to sing, I might just faint away."

Roger kept trying to time the spurts of the roaring to gaps in her conversation, but Eula was so excited about the Florida Folk Festival she couldn't stop talking. "I told Tom we had to get there early, get us a good spot up front," she said, while Roger revved up the saw with several sharp bursts. He heard ". . . little green plums . . ." and something about a red blanket, and she kept talking through the steady gnawing scream, and by the time the limb fell out, she was going on about Melvin and Tom.

". . . although Tom was his own son and you weren't even hardly a son-in-law—whoa, that was a big one, Roger, watch out. Tom just never had his heart in it, rather be outdoors. You're the one had a finger on that silver thread, Roger, Melvin always used to say that."

Roger had come into his music late in life. It wasn't until he was eighteen years old and courting Ethel that Ethel's uncle Melvin had begun to teach him to play. Melvin was a hard man in some ways, with dark parts of his life and secrets that no one talked about. But he was sweet in his music, and he patiently taught Roger his distinctive five-fingered picking style so thoroughly that by the time Roger learned that most people use only three or even two fingers, it was too late. "You was already rurnt!" Melvin told him.

Roger untangled a few twiggy branches stuck in the tree and climbed down with the chain saw. "You was already rurnt!" said Eula, brushing sawdust off his shoulders. "That was the way his daddy taught him to pick, Menominee style, he called it. He was so proud of you, Roger. You had a finger on that silver thread."

Eula and Tom were in the backyard adjusting the carburetor on his oldest truck.

"I was standing down there looking at those little green plums and thinking," said Eula.

"I said straight slot, not Phillips," said Tom.

" 'Just look at those little green plums,' I told Roger. 'By the time these plums are ripe, you'll be up on that marble stage picking and singing for thirty thousand people.' "

"I'm surprised you let him up in that tree with a chain saw," said Tom. "He could have cut off some of those precious fingers. Now get in and crank it, and keep it running this time."

"I told Roger we'd be there early, Tom," said Eula. "I told him to look out for a red blanket, a bright red spot among the thousands, and there we'd be, giving him encouragement to carry on."

"Since when did Roger ever need any encouragement to carry on?" said Tom. "I never knew Roger to stop till he got to the little piece of corn bread a-laying on the shelf. Now slack off on it."

"Well, he always did have—"

"I don't want to hear about that god-damned silver thread," said Tom, coming out from under the truck hood. "What gets me is, the Florida Folk Festival, 'Folk,' well, hell, Roger ain't folk. Roger's a Ph.D. doctor, a damned peanut expert. Just because he had the spare time to sit and listen to Daddy, and room in his head for forty-eleven verses of 'Frog Went a-Courtin',' that don't make him 'folk.' 'Folk' means you got your roots in poor soil your grandaddy wore out with cotton and a mule. You work with your hands, close to the dirt. Roger's family in that big house up there looking down on the rest of the county, just because the house burned down a generation ago, that don't make Roger 'folk.' Roger sits in front of a computer making spread-sheets all day and telling peanut farmers what to do with their land—he ain't all that different from his granddaddy, only Roger does it with education instead of money, it amounts to the same thing, and that ain't 'folk.' Now cut it off."

What could be closer to the dirt than peanuts, Eula thought, but she said, "He knows the words and the music, Tom, that's all they're after."

"And don't forget about that silver thread," said Tom, slamming down the hood of the truck and wiping his hands on a greasy rag.

"Women being murdered and thrown into rivers by jealous lovers," said Della, "and cuckoos and card players all mixed up, and houses filled with chicken pies. I don't know how Roger remembers the words, since there's no logic to it."

Della and Lucy were headed down State Road 41 to the Florida Folk Festival. Lucy was driving and Della was idly looking for birds in the woods and fields beside the road. The lavish spring flowering was finished, and rural north Florida was at its early summer best. The old live oak trees looked almost silly in their new green.

"The oldest songs have evolved away

from all reason and the words have just become part of the music," said Lucy. "You're not supposed to look for logic."

Della sat for a while with her hands in her lap, watching some mockingbirds chase a sparrow hawk. They drove through the little towns of Jasper and Genoa. There was not much traffic. The rest of the thirty thousand people going to the Florida Folk Festival were on the interstate.

"Will Ethel be there?" asked Della. "I'm afraid of Ethel. She's so quick-witted and strong, and she calls me 'that little bird woman.' "

"Ethel is staying home with Louise," said Lucy. "Ethel doesn't see the charm of folk music. She saw too much of her uncle Melvin and Roger, struggling along in those early years with fiddles and banjos and harmonicas."

"Roger never struggles," said Della.

"He doesn't appear to struggle," said Lucy, "because he handles his suffering so gracefully."

But Della was looking through her binoculars at a kingfisher on a fence post and didn't seem to hear.

* * *

"Sit down, Mama, you're making me nervous with those tomatoes," said Ethel. She was gluing the pieces of a broken chair back together in Eula's kitchen, and Louise was leaning on the sink, pushing Eula's first tomatoes back and forth on the windowsill.

"Where are they gone?" asked Louise. "Eula told me, but I forgot."

"They're all down in Florida listening to Roger play 'I Wish I Was a Mole in the Ground' to a throng of thousands," said Ethel.

"And Melvin will play 'The Waxful Maid,'" said Louise.

"Melvin's dead, Mama," said Ethel. "Been dead."

"Eula told me that, but I forgot," said Louise.

"Yeah, well, your mind was on other things," said Ethel.

"Roger had his finger on that silver thread," said Louise. "That's what Melvin always says."

"We can never forget that, can we?" said Ethel.

Then Louise sat in a chair and clasped

her hands together on the kitchen table and began to sing. " 'Down on her knees before him, she pleaded for her life,' " she sang in a husky voice, way too low to manage anything like a tune. " 'But deep into her bosom he plunged the fatal knife.' "

"What do you want for lunch, Mama, fried tomatoes or okra and tomatoes? I'm cooking," said Ethel.

But Louise had a finger on that silver thread. She couldn't stop. She sat straight up in the chair, and with such an intent look in her eyes that they almost seemed to cross, she sang, " 'Oh, Willie, my poor darling, why have you taken my life? I've always loved you, Willie, and wanted to be your wife.' "

"Jesus, Mama," said Ethel.

" 'I never have deceived you,' " sang Louise, " 'and with my parting breath, I will forgive you, Willie, and close my eyes in death.' "

"Thank goodness," said Ethel. "Now tell me what you want to eat, tomatoes or okra."

"I am reminded of maggots," said Meade, "when you turn over a rotting carcass with a stick and see the mass of maggots squirm." And from the high point at the entrance to the Stephen Foster Folk Culture Center where Meade and Hilma were waiting, the crowd did have a squirmy look, milling around with small movements. A cluster of about five hundred were clumped around the food tents eating fried dough and Polish sausages; a little wriggling knot of a hundred or so crowded together at the crafts exhibit watching an old man weaving a split-oak basket and an old Seminole woman sewing bits of bright cloth together on a treadle-powered sewing machine; and another undulating crowd with ever-changing edges nudged itself up against the row of portable toilets.

"Or aphids," said Hilma, peering through her balled-up fists at the swatches of color.

"Maggots!" said Meade, and then Della and Lucy arrived with two folding aluminum chairs. "Just in case we might need to sit down and rest," said Lucy, using the tactful "we."

"Maggots?" said Della.

"I would like to sit down," said Hilma,

sinking gratefully into a chair. "You are so wise, Lucy."

"Now where is Roger, do you think?" she asked, and they all shaded their eyes and peered down into the crowd.

" 'Consumed by that which it was nourished by,' " said Meade.

Now where has Tom gone off to? thought Eula. He had helped her spread out the red blanket, but then he had started talking to a man about a junk car, and since then such a crowd had gathered, she was afraid he would never find her again. There was a family with two babies on her left, and a young couple on her right smelling so much like coconuts that it made her sneeze, and beyond them in front and behind all she could see was people's faces and backs and towels and blankets and quilts covering up the hillside. Several blankets that she could see were red, and that worried her. What if Roger looked out in a weak moment, seeking the comfort of a friendly face, maybe if he got lost for a second after "I wish I was a lizard in the spring" and could only find the faces of strangers on red blankets, he might falter. But then suddenly there was Lucy, sitting down beside her and offering her a bottle of drinking water, and she began to feel better.

"Tom went off with a fat man with a tattoo on his arm," Eula told her, "talking about car engines. It might have been a mermaid or a submarine. But Tom has been talking so bad about music lately anyway, and Roger's peanut work—spreadsheets and not being close to the dirt, I'd rather he did have his mind on carburetors than music."

Then Lucy invited Eula to come and sit with her and Hilma and Meade "so you won't be all by yourself if Tom doesn't come back."

But Eula didn't quite like the idea of sitting with Meade. She could have such a cold look sometimes, and a sharp way of speaking. Way across the hill, at the far edge of the crowd, beyond the crawling babies and rowdy teenagers and hot pregnant women flapping the tails of their shirts up and down and entire families on quilts eating meals out of Styrofoam containers, Eula could see Meade sitting up straight in a chair. She was gazing placidly down into the woods by the river as if she would not be surprised to see a prince dressed all in white and gold come up the banks of the Suwannee and take her away in a glass carriage.

"No," said Eula, "I'd better wait here for Tom on this red blanket."

The spray was not turned on in the fountain, and there was just enough water in the pool for the frog to swim easily. Every time she thrust forward with her back legs, long streamers of eggs would flow out behind her, shining black dots encased in clear gel. There would be the smooth thrust and an angled glide, the undulating streamers of eggs would swirl, and then the frog's back feet would relax gently and the streamers would settle peacefully in spirals and loops. It had to be the most graceful egg laying in the world, Della thought. She squatted by the fountain with her arms on the lip of the pool, mesmerized by gleam and shine and glide.

"Mama, come see!"

"Look at this frog laying eggs!"

"Oooh, gross!"

"Come look, there's two of them!"

But Della didn't hear the voices of the people who strolled past the fountain, and she didn't hear the amplified voice as it drifted through the park from the Old Marble Stage:

". . . from up in Georgia . . ."

". . . in the tradition of . . ."

". . . please welcome . . ."

She just squatted there with the glistening colors in the spring sunlight and the bowl of bright water, sunk under the spell of this elegant fecundity.

"A good generator and starter, good compression, he wants a hundred dollars for it," said Tom. "In Jasper."

In spite of all the red blankets, Roger had spotted her right away, Eula thought. He had given her a little smile and a wink. Even from that distance she had been sure of it. Why in the world is that old woman crying over "I Wish I Was a Mole in the Ground"? She guessed everybody sitting around her had wondered that. It was probably just the excitement, being far from home and all by herself among so many strangers, and the memory of Roger, just a boy in those days, with a full head of hair, and the way Melvin would get that light look in his eyes when he came in, and how Roger would listen so hard and then nod and say "Yessir," and try out something new. They would sit so close their knees would almost touch, not really ever singing and playing much, just going over and over one little thing or another.

"I'd have to haul it, it don't run, he told me that up front. It's a parts car. The steering sector alone would cost me over a hundred dollars out at Jack's."

Melvin was sweet in his music, Eula thought, and she was glad it was dark on this long ride home from the Florida Folk Festival, and that Tom was talking about cars.

"Talking! And slurping on that blue drink!" said Meade. "During the music! I can only hope that from that distance Roger didn't notice. If I could have found a stick, I would have beat them with it."

"Oh, Meade," said Hilma. She was tired, and she couldn't stop thinking about Della, so captivated by copulating frogs she had missed the whole performance—the setting sun, the marble stage with the river behind it, and Roger

up there in front of all those people looking so dignified, playing a dead man's
music just as it ought to be played. It was
only after a parks official had scooped
the frogs out of the pool with a long-
handled net that Della had come to join
them. By then Roger had finished and
people were gathering up their blankets
and their children, and two barefooted
men with ponytails and a wet black dog
had begun playing Frisbee on the side of
the hill.

"Why do they go to a music festival if
they don't care enough to listen to the
music?" said Meade, and Hilma said
wearily, "Oh, Meade, people hardly ever
behave the way we wish they would."

23. THE ANVIL OF EXPERIENCE

The first thing Roger saw on Saturday morning was a dead broad-headed skink, a fine big male, sunk to the bottom of two gallons of peanut oil on his side porch. It was lying on its back in the fish cooker, its little front feet crossed peacefully over its pale belly.

"She has left me for the birds of the southern hemisphere," Roger said to himself, "and now this." He stood for a minute in his nightshirt, looking at the dead skink. "Got in, couldn't get out. Drowned in peanut oil," he said. He fished the skink out with a stick and threw it in the bushes where a cat would get it. It was a sad start to the day.

"He put her on the airplane to Australia on Friday afternoon and then he had to go right home and give that fish fry for Dean Rufus Routhe," said Meade.

"Poor Roger," said Hilma, "having to entertain agricultural scientists and fry fish with a broken heart in the setting sun, all the time thinking about Della, three miles up in the sky and halfway around the world, never to return."

But "never to return" had a rather melodramatic ring to it. Knowing Della, it would not be anything as deliberately final as that. Her mind would settle on first one thing and then another, and it would be merely a series of whims that would gradually draw her farther and farther away from Roger and the brief south Georgia part of her life. Still, everyone had the feeling that Della was gone, and would stay gone.

Hilma was the first to call Roger up and invite him for a meal. It was very strong, clear chicken soup, twice cooked, she said, toast, a salad, and a delicate custard for dessert. The kind of food that might be prepared for an invalid, Roger thought.

The subjects of Della, all species of birds, and the entire southern hemisphere were scrupulously avoided, and Hilma feigned an extraordinary interest in the career of Dr. Rufus Routhe, who was retiring as dean of the plant pathology department. Roger noticed a pale spot on the wall where Hilma had taken down a Menoboni print of crested flycatchers, as if she thought a picture of birds might cause him pain. She encouraged him to talk about peanuts, the hard summer of work ahead, and his duties in the next year as president of the southern division of the American Phytopathological Society. Roger told her about a new peanut cultivar, 'Georgia Routhe,' named in honor of the retiring dean, which had shown some resistance to TSWV. "Peanuts in the U.S. are usually named for scientists," he said, "but in Australia they are named for artists."

Hilma's eyes flew to the pale spot on the wall, and she began rattling dishes and talking wildly about Dean Routhe, until at last Roger stopped her and said,

"You really don't have to be this careful, Hilma." After that she put down the dishes with relief and seemed to relax, and for the rest of the evening they talked quite comfortably about the courtship display of the superb lyrebird ("excessive," said Hilma), Della's character ("flighty," said Hilma), and love.

"I don't quite understand the demands of that kind of love," said Hilma. "All those feelings were so long ago, the opportunities were so limited then, and we had different rules." But, she said, she had noticed how so often it left its victims ragged and spent, and she wondered why sensible people allowed themselves to begin, knowing where it would lead.

"There is no beginning to love," Roger said. "It just creeps over you."

"Oh," said Hilma, "like brown rot on a plum tree in the dark winter months, and by the time you become aware of it, the leaves are out and it's too late to spray."

"Yes," said Roger, "just like that. Now let me help you hang your flycatchers back on the wall." And Hilma got him a chair and fetched the Menoboni print from where she had hidden it in the closet.

* * *

The next morning Roger had to get up at 4:30 and drive all the way down to Atta-pulgus to hoe out the alleys in the peanut test plots there and then turn around and drive in the other direction all the way up to Plains to mark ailing plants and collect leaf and flower samples. He had a rattle-snake scare in the morning, and he ran into a wasp nest in an aluminum gate in the afternoon and got stung twice. Meade had invited him to supper, but when he went home to change clothes, Eula was standing in his yard holding three chickens by the feet, two big red hens and a rooster.

"Roger," she said, "you didn't know it because you was up there at UNC, but when Melvin was killed by his own Allis-Chalmers tractor I found a lot of comfort in chickens." The chickens slowly spun in her grasp, their wings limp, their beaks open in an expression of wonderment and resignation. "Rhode Island Reds, Roger," said Eula. "I thought Dominickers would be—well, they might bring back memories, Roger, and I hate to see you sad." She thrust the chickens' trussed-up feet into his hands and hugged him tight, mashing a strangled squawk out of one of the hens. Then she quickly turned away, got into her car, and drove off in a hurry, so that Roger wouldn't see her tears.

Roger made a waterer out of a jar and a dish and a toothpick, spread newspapers on the floor of his back porch, and then turned the chickens loose, washed his hands and face, and arrived at Meade's house a half hour late, drugged on antihistamine, with the grit of dried sweat under his clothes, and the sand from the Plains peanut fields in his shoes, worrying about regulations regarding livestock within the city limits.

Meade sat him down on the sofa, made him comfortable, and then stood in front of him waving a silver serving spoon in the air. "Roger," she said, "you must hammer out your life on the anvil of experience!"

But Roger was too tired and sleepy to think of a reply to this violent piece of advice. Every time he closed his eyes he saw green leaves, as if overexposure had stamped an image of a field of peanut plants on the backs of his eyeballs.

"You do choose the most difficult women, Roger," Meade went on. "First Ethel, so wild and independent, and then Della—a gifted artist, but aside from that she was—"

"I don't choose them, Meade," said Roger, through a confusion of weariness. "They creep over me like brown rot."

The next day the Coastal Plain Experiment Station was putting on the Ag Showcase. Booths presenting information on different agricultural topics had been set up on the grounds: "Red Imported Fire Ants: Friend or Foe?," "Animal Waste Awareness," "Biocontrol of Musk Thistle." Food was being served from portable carts, and staff members were giving tours of the soybean and corn variety tests, the oldest pecan cultivar trial in the world (1921), and the new controlled-atmosphere Vidalia Onion Storage Lab. The public was invited, which meant that there would be a lot of questions about potted geraniums and what to do about those big green worms on tomato plants.

This was Dean Routhe's last Ag

Showcase, and all morning he had been flapping around the Bermuda grass germ plasm plot and the Vidalia Onion Storage Lab like a lanky old crane. Dean Routhe was not the kind of scientist who should be turned loose in a crowd; he was apt to frighten people by suddenly blurting out bits of abstruse information. No one quite knew what to do. After all, a peanut cultivar had been named for this man.

"Get him in there with Roger," said Dr. Vanlandingham desperately, and so, by midmorning Dean Routhe had settled down in the booth on Predictive Models of Peanut Diseases, where he kept hurling out random remarks about agronomy, entomology, and the virtues of matrimony.

"Men need wives!" he cried out in a high, carrying voice, interrupting Roger's little talk about the future of Georgia's peanut crop. Roger faltered, then soldiered on.

"—the entomologists studying the thrips vectors—"

"Men need wives!" called Dean Routhe.

"—the virologists comparing TSWV

with other, better-understood diseases," Roger continued stalwartly.

"Look at this!" cried Dean Routhe, springing up out of the shadowy back of the booth. "My hair was red when I began my work here at the CPES in '59!" He clutched a few strands of white hair with both hands. "But my wife died in '65, and within a year it turned snow white!"

"—and my own work with—"

"Men need wives!" said Dean Routhe, clapping an arm around Roger's shoulder and glaring out at the stricken crowd. Roger could feel the old gnarly fingers trembling against his back. A few people hastily replaced the pamphlets and peanut brochures they had taken from the shelf, and very quickly everyone scurried off to the next booth, "Our Friend the Dairy Cow."

"Dean Routhe," said Roger, "maybe you would like to—"

But Dean Routhe was busily pulling up two chairs. "Roger," he said, "sit down." And they both sat down and faced each other across their knees.

"Roger," said Dean Routhe in a deep, throbbing voice, "she's left you. She's gone. GONE." He paused. "But you must not sit back and moan and pine. You've got to have a fearless heart, Roger, a FEARLESS heart!" and he thumped his own rickety chest so hard that Roger tensed up and leaned forward slightly.

"Roger," said Dean Routhe, "it's like falling off a horse. The best thing you can do is just get right back up in that saddle again. Back in the saddle again."

Outside, a new crowd had begun to gather. Some in the front were leafing through the pamphlets on the plywood shelf in a businesslike way, but they kept sneaking glances into the dark interior of the booth, and at the back of the crowd people were staring in at Roger and Dean Routhe, their mouths hanging slightly open.

"Dean Routhe," Roger whispered.

"Oh, quite so, quite so!" said Dean Routhe, scrambling to his feet and addressing the crowd. "You listen to this fine young man," he said to a pretty, frightened-looking red-haired woman in a black John Birch Society T-shirt. "You ask him any question about the plants in your home or in your garden or on your small farm. Nematology, the rusts, myco-toxins—why, this man is an expert on late blight of potato!" he said, and he grabbed Roger by both arms and thrust him forward. "What this young man doesn't know about foliar diseases of peanut wouldn't fit into a teacup! A TEACUP!"

In the late afternoon a little stage was set up in the middle of the millet trials for a musical performance, and a half acre was roped off for dancing. Roger played the banjo; Tim Bannister, his entomologist counterpart in the TSWV research, played fiddle; and a couple of paid musicians from Tifton played guitars. In the cool of the evening, after the sun went down, people began to dance on the smooth turf of the Bermuda grass germ plasm plot. Dean Routhe had taken hold of the notion that the harvesting of crops was inherently violent, and he kept accosting people and saying, "Everything you eat has been attacked by someone!"

Roger noticed with dismay that the red-haired woman in the black T-shirt was watching him and edging closer and closer to the stage, an odd, almost rapturous look on her face, and he played faster and faster, running "The Blind Girl" right up against "Pig in a Pen." He remembered Meade's remark about the anvil of experience, but all he could think of was the dead skink in the peanut oil, its little toes curled up, its little eyes closed, and its broad jowls, even in death, still tinged with the breeding orange.

24. QUITE A YEAR FOR PLUMS

"Quite a year for plums," everybody kept saying, but that didn't begin to describe the plum crop of that early summer. A rare combination of favorable factors had contributed to it, the fruit scientists said: a warm early spring had brought out the honeybees when the trees were flowering, then in March and April it had rained twice a week as the little plums grew, and finally at fruit swell the weather turned hot and dry, discouraging brown rot. Now in June heavy laden limbs drooped and cracked off, and in every household people were eating plums and baking cakes with plums, cooking up plum jam and plum jelly, or just raking up mounds and piles of rotten plums, and getting stung by yellow jackets. Drunken birds whopsided from eating fermented plums staggered across lawns. Then an unseasonable heat wave came through, in early June when no one was prepared for it, and standing over hot stoves boiling down plum juice, everybody started remembering stories about the tragedy of 1903, when five people in Perote had died of heat exhaustion.

"My father always said how peaceful Mr. Loomis looked, lying there flat on his back in the bed in the front room under the open window, dead as a stone with the thin sheet pulled up to his chin," said Meade. Her father, just a little boy then, had been the one to find the body of Mr. Loomis, a timber baron who had made a fortune shipping longleaf cants out of Carrabelle to be resawn in the Netherlands. "People knew how to die back in those days," said Meade.

Hilma didn't know if it was just the heat, or if it was Jim Wade's endless tinkering with a fan he had brought to blow on her while she made plum jelly, or what it was exactly that was making her irritable. "They didn't know how to die any better than we do," she snapped at Meade. "They just told it better."

"There's something about a fan, blowing on a dead person," said Jim Wade, staring contemplatively at a little pile of worm gears. "When you think how the fingers that turned on that switch at bedtime will never again . . ." Meade's father had never mentioned a fan in his many tellings of the story of the Loomis death; just the thin sheet pulled up to Mr. Loomis's very prominent chin had stuck in his mind. But now as she looked at the bucket of plum seeds and plum skins and the jelly bag dripping plum juice into the bowl in Hilma's sink, another part of the story came back to Meade, something that she had almost forgotten, because over the years the thin sheet had become the hinge of the story: her father had been taking a bucket of plums to old Mr. Loomis. Meade sat down heavily in Hilma's kitchen chair and rested her chin in her hands. "A bucket of plums," she whispered.

"Honey, at the plums!" Eula said to Ethel, flapping her apron in delight. Andy and the plum crop had come on the same weekend, and it was almost more than Eula could stand. She kept running back and forth between the jelly pot on the stove and the backyard, where Andy was practicing breathing through a snorkel. Roger had promised to take him to Ammonia Spring to swim with the manatees when he got back from his phytopathology meeting in Austin, Texas, and every waking minute since he had arrived yesterday afternoon, Andy had been stalking around the house with a bright pink and purple face mask on, making moist snorting sounds. Eula kept looking for the ravages of the brown rice and date diet. He was thinner, she thought, but then he was taller too. She hadn't really been able to get a good look at his face.

"Look at the plums under that tree, Ethel, did you ever—" But Ethel had set down the boxes of quart jars on the kitchen table and run out into the yard. She grabbed Andy up in both arms and hugged him too tight, knocking his face mask crooked. When she finally turned him loose he had to pick his ears out from under the rubber straps and get another grip on the snorkel with his poor stretched-out lips. "I'hh ynh uh ahhys wryds wid Roger," he said, and Ethel squatted down in front of him, held him by both arms, and peered in eagerly through the face mask at his bugged-out eyes and his stretched-flat nose. "You're going to Ammonia Spring with Roger, I heard that," she said, and she hugged him again, more carefully this time.

"Just because nobody ever saw a manatee eat somebody alive, they think they never do it," Tom called down. He was painting Cool Seal on Louise's roof, but the tar was so hot and runny it wouldn't stick.

"What are you doing up in the air, Tom?" called Louise. "Come down from there."

"You're dripping on the azalea bushes, Tom," called Ethel.

"They're vegetarians, Daddy, they don't eat people. I read it in *Ranger Rick*," called Andy.

"Yeah right," said Tom. "Did you know that a living giant squid has never been seen by human eyes? But that don't mean they're not down there."

"Human eyes," said Louise.

"Here I am sending my only son out to Ammonia Spring and you're going to come back with both your legs gnawed off," said Tom.

"I'll be all right, Daddy," called Andy, and he wrapped his lips back around the snorkel.

"Well, all I can say is, rub some spit around in your mask to keep it from fogging up, so you can see them when they start coming after you," said Tom.

Roger's seat mate had talked quite brightly during the first half of the flight, sipping ginger ale and telling him about the meeting she had attended in Austin, something to do with funding for community colleges. Then, "And what took you to Texas?" she asked. Roger said, "It was a meeting of plant scientists"—only that, but next thing he knew she had fallen asleep and was slumping over onto his shoulder, drooling a little, with her hand flopped against his thigh. He tried to squirm out from under her, but he was trapped in the window seat with nowhere to go; every time he shifted she just snuggled closer. She would be embarrassed when she woke up, he knew that. Two seats up and across the aisle he could see Lucy sitting in the exit row, reading a paper about parasitic wasps and cereal leaf beetles quite coolly, with all the space in the world. Finally he gave up and just stared out the window at the black night and the little twinkling lights of towns down below.

"We are beginning our descent into . . ." said the voice. "Please—" and suddenly the woman sprang upright, clamped both arms across her chest, and stared wildly at Roger and then at the seat back in front of her.

"You're all right," said Roger. "You just fell asleep, that's all." He helped her get her bag out of the overhead compartment and watched her scamper down the aisle away from him, teetering on her high-heeled shoes. He gathered up his briefcase and he and Lucy walked together through the little airport and out to his truck in the parking lot, and then drove off down the lit-up streets of Tallahassee. They talked for a while about a genetically engineered baculovirus they'd learned about in Austin; it had been very effective in controlling cotton bollworms and tobacco budworms in field tests. Then they talked about the heat and the plums and the trip to Ammonia Spring.

"Meade can't stop thinking about the five deaths in Perote in '03," said Lucy.

"I wonder how many dozen quarts of jam Eula has put up?" said Roger.

"I wonder if Andy has once turned loose of that snorkel since he's been here," said Lucy.

They drove past the shopping centers on the edge of town, and the new subdivisions with their fancy entrances, and the last Publix Supermarket, lit up in a blaze of light like the promised land. Then suddenly Lucy said, "You're a good man, Roger."

But Roger couldn't think of anything to say to that, and they just drove on in the dark without talking anymore, past the cotton fields and the peanut fields and the woodpecker woods to home.

ACKNOWLEDGMENTS

For their help and advice, I would like to thank the American Livestock Breeds Conservancy, Wilson Baker, Polly Blackford, Brandy Cowley, Ken Crawford, Albert Culbreath, the Dominique Club of America, Steve Earle, Todd Engstrom, Jeanne Greenleaf, Rosalie Hawkins Olson, Robert O. Hawse, Katharine Heath, Paul Hjort, Daryle Jennette, Nell Johnson, Beck Johnston, Jonathon Lazear, Mary Lawrence Lilly, Roy Lilly III, Frank Lindamood, June Bailey McDaniel, Eula McGraw, Bruce McIntosh, O. Victor Miller, Red Parham, Lance Rockwell, Sonny Sammons, Sigrid Sanders, Gordon Scott, Sonny Stoddard, Carl Tomlinson, Barbara White, Jane White, Robb White, John Witt, Ron Yrabedra, and Coleman Zuber.